NIGHT PILOT

Library of Congress Cataloging-in-Publication Data

Tilton, Lynn, 1941–
    Night pilot / by Lynn and Jane Tilton.
      p. cm.
    Summary: When a football injury leaves Matt bitter, he learns an important lesson about trusting people and the Lord after becoming friends with a pilot and learning how to fly
    ISBN 0-87579-384-3
    [1. Airplanes — Fiction. 2. Flight — Fiction. 3. Mormons — Fiction. 4. Christian life — Fiction.]   I. Tilton, Jane, 1943–
II. Title.
PZ7.T472Ni   1991
[Fic] — dc20   91-6739
                                                    CIP
                                                     AC

Printed in the United States of America

10   9   8   7   6   5   4   3   2   1

NIGHT PILOT

LYNN AND JANE TILTON

Deseret Book Company
Salt Lake City, Utah

1

MATT HANSEN LAY NEAR THE GOAL LINE and knew the agony of disaster. First-string running back for the Cumberland Ridge High School Indians, Matt had dreamed of his senior season for years. He'd be scouted; he'd win his scholarship, just as his dad had done. It was the next ticket to punch toward his goal of pro football. This Labor Day practice was only a scrimmage, the last big practice before the opening game, but his season was all over now. He'd made his last play.

It wasn't just the pain. He'd endured pain over the years as he worked single-mindedly to become a great running back. Matt started playing football when he still was too young for Cub Scouts. After his father died, the sport was his only link with his dad. He read football stories. He lifted weights. He ran. He played Midget ball, Little League football, junior-high ball. He made the varsity team his sophomore year. Now he knew that it was over. And Bill "Beef" Kowalski, his own team's top defensive lineman, had done him in.

Matt tried to get up. Waves of pain swirled over him. No matter how he ignored the pain, his leg wouldn't hold him. He sank back onto the grass, defeated. He'd been warned. Twice, Kowalski had told him, "Cool it, Hansen. Without the rest of us, you're nothing. Zero!"

Matt chalked it up to jealousy. His name had appeared frequently in the local papers last year. There'd been a big feature recently, predicting that Matt Hansen would lead the Indians to All-State.

Cumberland Ridge employed a running game, and Matt was a star among the stars on the top-ranked high school team. In his junior year, he'd made the Pennsylvania team for the North-South game against Maryland's finest high-school ball players.

His troubles with Kowalski began last year when Matt referred to Kowalski and his fellow linemen as "a bunch of Rambos, big on beef, small on brains," after a badly bungled play that led to Cumberland Ridge's only loss of the season. The nickname "Beef" stuck, and Kowalski didn't like it, especially since he had to be tutored in math.

Kowalski had finally gotten his revenge. Toward the end of practice, Coach Robbins had called for a goal-line defense. Matt took the ball on a short pitch by the quarterback and plunged for the line. Kowalski roared past his man and charged for Matt's knees. Wilson, one of Beef's friends, came from the left, striking high.

Matt's right leg, stretched at the tackle, took the weight of a quarter ton of angry players before bending the wrong way. Matt twisted to lessen the impact when Wilson plowed over him, but his knee couldn't take the punishment. A couple of other players piled on top, and Matt screamed in agony.

Coach Robbins bulled into the melee immediately, huge hands jerking players off the pile. "Get the rest of these burros on the bleachers," he told his assistant. "This is a scrimmage; save the rough stuff for Friday.

"You okay, Hansen?"

"Yeah," Matt lied. He tried again to get up, but he couldn't make his leg hold him.

Coach Robbins ordered an ambulance. "Don't try to get up again, Hansen." Coach Robbins broke open an ice pack and wrapped it around Matt's knee. The icy coolness brought some relief. By the time the ambulance arrived, the pain had numbed to a dull ache.

Matt felt foolish when the stretcher bearers ran onto the field. He tried to stand. Halfway up he fell, nearly losing consciousness from the white-hot surge of pain. He let the men strap him down.

The coach jumped into the ambulance with him. "Call his family," he ordered his equipment manager.

By the time Matt's mother arrived at the hospital, Dr. Jackson, the orthopedic surgeon, had completed his inspection. X-rays were clipped to the light table.

"When can I go home, Dr. Jackson?" Matt knew the answer, but he had to hear it from someone else.

"As soon as you recuperate from surgery."

"But school starts tomorrow. I've got a game Friday!"

Dr. Jackson looked at the x-rays again. "Matt, if the surgery goes well, and if you take care of your leg, you may be able to play ball again. Next year."

"Dr. Jackson, if I don't play this year, I won't get a scholarship. A walk-on doesn't stand a chance. If I can't play college ball, I'll never make the pros."

Nancy Hansen put her arm around her son. Her voice was soft, but her face was grim, "Matt, life's tough, but we don't have to face it alone. I'll call the bishop and ask him to give you a blessing." She turned to the doctor. "His office is only a couple of blocks from here."

"Forget it!" Matt said. "It's too late."

"Matt's always wanted to play pro ball," Nancy explained apologetically. "His father played college ball. He'd have been a professional football player if it hadn't been for Vietnam. Matt's always wanted to be like him."

"My father's lucky—he's dead!" Matt shouted. His face went blank as he shut out the world around him.

Through the fog, Little Matt took the handoff and charged to the right. An opposing lineman crashed into him, but Matt

3

caught himself before he fell and ran across the line of scrimmage. He made over ten yards before he was tackled from behind.

The jar rattled his teeth. Tears came to his eyes. Big boys don't cry. That's what his daddy said. He refused to let the tightness in his chest come out as he jogged to the huddle for the next play.

After the Bluejays won their game, he trotted over to his waiting father. Big Matt, sharply dressed in his Air Force blues, clapped him on the back. "I'm proud of you, Son. Great game! You'll make more yards next time."

Someday Matt would run all the way to the goal line, and his father would be there, watching him. Someday his efforts would be enough. His dad would say, "Good job, Matt!"

Matt swirled out of the fog into the recovery room. He looked down at the sheet covering his legs. Moving them took too much effort. Matt drifted back under the anesthesia.

An Air Force pilot who had done three tours in Vietnam, back to back, Big Matt was a hero to Little Matt's friends. Periodically, his dad took Matt's friends to the base and showed them the F-15 he flew. The boys sat in the pilot's seat and tried the controls.

Then the group trouped over to the reception center to watch flying films. Little Matt imagined his hand on the throttle. The control wheel slid smoothly back, and Little Matt lifted the plane off the runway, hurtling into the sky. The whole world got heavy, just as Dad described it.

Those were the best of times, especially when they met Big Matt's buddies. Big Matt had married just after his mission, while he was still in college. None of the other pilots had a boy as old as Matt. "I'm going to be a pilot just like you, Dad," he'd say in front of his dad's friends. Big Matt would clap him on the back and grin.

The anesthesia wore off. Two orderlies wheeled him to his room. His mom was waiting. She looked scared.

"How long was I in there, Mom?"

"Quite a lot longer than they expected. But Dr. Jackson says you'll be fine. He thinks you'll play ball again someday."

The orderlies helped Matt move from the gurney to his bed. They handled his leg carefully but firmly. His mother sat in the bedside chair trying to look cheerful.

"I'm awful tired, Mom," he said. He closed his eyes and drifted off again.

The worst part of military life is saying good-bye. The Hansens moved several times after Big Matt's return from Vietnam. Moves meant promotion—"ticket punching," Big Matt called it. After Vietnam, fighter pilots were surplus. Matt's dad held a commission in the Reserve. He was always in danger of being pushed into the civilian world if he didn't make rank on time.

"You got to get your ticket punched in the right places," he'd tell Nancy and Little Matt. "If you do, you'll go to the top." The top was where he intended to be. Anywhere else was nowhere.

Ticket punching meant periodic separations too. They said good-bye again to Big Matt. This time he was on temporary duty, TDY, in Arizona, flying experimental versions of the F-15 over the gunnery ranges of the southern Arizona desert.

Matt's mother was frightened. "It's only ninety days, Nan. I'll be back before the baby's born."

"Matt, we've already lost two babies. I don't think I can handle losing another one without you here. Do you have to go?"

"You know how hard it is to make rank since the end of the war. It's either up or out."

Nothing could be worse. Matt was old enough to realize that being a fighter pilot made his dad one of an elite group. There was an unconscious arrogance in the fighter pilots. They looked on the rest of the service as their support personnel. Flying those planes was what was really important.

So they said good-bye to Big Matt. A horn honked. Big Matt picked up his suitcase and opened the door. He gave Nancy a hard hug, shook Little Matt's hand. "You take good care of your mom. You're the man of the family while I'm gone."

Nancy clung to her husband.

"Don't worry, Nan. Everything'll be fine. I'll get down to Nogales and bring you something back." He took her by the shoulders, squeezed quickly, and set her aside. Big Matt ran down the steps, crossed the yard, and stepped into the waiting van. He didn't look back.

Matt looked up at his mother, who was wiping tears from her eyes. He'd never seen her cry. "When dad gets his star, he'll never have to leave us. He'll be base commander, and he can stay home."

Nancy Hansen looked into her son's earnest face. "Your dad wants that star very badly. We want it for him, Matt. We have to let him go."

"Maybe this is the last time," the boy said.

It was. Three weeks later, the base chaplain appeared on the doorstep. Nancy Hansen answered the door with a smile. It faded when she saw the bishop standing with him. The we-regret-to-inform-you that she had lived in dread of hearing through three long years during the Vietnam conflict had finally come.

"Major Hansen's plane crashed last night during exercises over the Copper Mountains east of Yuma. I was notified as soon as the search crew reached the plane. I'm terribly sorry."

The chaplain left, but the bishop stayed until they got a final report. The plane had burned on the mountainside. Major Hansen's body was sealed inside a flag-draped military casket and flown home for the funeral.

Matt never liked to remember those days. The Relief Society brought food. They insisted his mother stay in bed. Matt didn't realize that the ward was afraid she would lose the baby as well.

He stood with his mother and the bishop at the graveside. The twenty-one-gun salute echoed away. The officer in charge handed the folded flag to his mother. There was an aching emptiness in the pit of Matt's stomach. He never wanted to see a plane again.

On a sunny day not quite three months later, Matt's brother, John, was born. After his mother had returned from the hospital, the bishop visited. "Sister Hansen, have you made plans to move?"

"I've decided to make a real break. We're going to Pennsylvania."

"Why Pennsylvania?"

"It just feels right. We did a tour there just before Matt was born — Matt was in charge of recruiting. He hated not flying, but we loved Pennsylvania. Matt always planned to retire there."

"What about your family, Sister Hansen? Wouldn't you rather go home?"

"I'm an Army brat, Bishop. My folks are in Southern California now. I'm not close to my mom, and I hate the Coast."

"What about living near Matt's folks in Idaho? It might be good for the boys."

"I've thought of that too. But Matt never wanted to go back. I want to live where Matt wanted to be." That was the end of the discussion.

Visiting teachers cleaned and packed. Home teachers crated belongings for the move. Big Matt's buddies came once or twice, but they couldn't afford to look back. Matt's death could happen to any of them. Little Matt didn't want to be around pilots anymore. He and his mother clung together.

The bishop was concerned about them. "Money won't be a problem," Nancy told him. "My pension as a major's widow is adequate, and Matt believed in insurance. We can buy a home. I won't have to work while the boys are home. If there's anything good about all this, that's it."

"Sister Hansen, I'm not going to preach the gospel to you. You understand as well as I do that there'll be hard times ahead. You won't always want to, but you'll get the strength you need to handle them. The Lord who saw the sparrow fall saw Matt go down. He won't leave you alone, but you'll have to seek him. Teach your boys to look for him. They'll need him too."

When they moved to Pennsylvania, Matt threw himself into football. He got his ticket punched in all the right places as he worked toward his father's dream. Now his ticket had been bent, folded, spindled, and mutilated.

Matt awoke thirsty. He reached for the cup of ice chips on the bedside table. His mother crossed the room to help.

"You going to stay all night, Mom?"

"How do you feel, Matt?"

"I'm okay, just sleepy."

She picked up her purse. "I wanted to be sure you were all right, but I'd better get home. John will want to know how you are. I'll be back after supper, and Bishop Adams said he'd drop over after he made another call this evening."

She stopped in the doorway and looked back. "You'll make it, Matt. You're too much like your father not to."

Matt switched TV channels aimlessly, trying to take his mind off his knee. His football career was over. Dr. Jackson said he might be able to play next year, but next year was too late. No college scout would find him sitting on the bench. Coaches avoided injury-prone players. What were his chances as a walk-on? Without a scholarship, his chances were almost nothing. He'd just have to accept it.

A tall, thin nurse's aide walked in with a fresh bowl of ice chips. She looked only two or three years older than Matt. "Hi, I'm Marie." She handed him the bowl of chips. Matt spooned a couple into his mouth. "I'm so glad the operation was a success," Marie said. "My family used to watch you play. My cousin's a lineman, Bill Kowalski. I'll bet he's a friend of yours."

Matt choked on the ice chip, coughing it out. The ice bounced on the sheet and landed on the floor.

Marie scooped the chip off the floor and threw it into the bedpan. "Is there anything else I can get you?"

Matt shook his head.

"I'll be back with your supper."

Matt sagged back on his pillows. Never had he felt so helpless. He glanced at the expectant bedpan — and turned on the TV. He tried to escape into it.

He didn't want to watch sports. He hated soaps, and he couldn't stand the pseudo-excitement of game shows. After flipping through the channels, he gave up. Under the magazines his mother left were several well-read ones the Candy Striper had brought. Among them was a dog-eared flight magazine. Matt hadn't read about flying since his dad died. He started to toss the magazine away, then shrugged his shoulders and began flipping slowly through the pages.

Midway through *Adventures in Flight,* Marie appeared with his supper. She cranked Matt's bed up and swung the table across. She removed the metal cover from the plate and left Matt to his dinner. He wasn't hungry. He poked listlessly through the meatloaf, the vegetable medley, and didn't even try the bread pudding.

Marie returned for the tray. "You'll have to do better than

9

that if you want Dr. Jackson to let you out of here. Football players need lots of energy."

"I'm not a football player anymore," Matt snapped.

"Sor-ry." Marie left the room.

Not a minute later there was a knock on the door. "Hi, Matt," Bishop Adams said cheerfully. He carried a wrapped box in his left hand. Bishop Adams pulled a chair over to the bedside. "Matt, I can't even begin to tell you how sorry I was when your mother called me. How'd the surgery go?"

"Just fine," he responded tonelessly.

Bishop Adams looked at him closely. "You mean 'the operation was a success, but the patient died'?"

"I'm fine, Bishop."

"You're lying, Matt."

His blunt reply shocked Matt, although the bishop had a reputation for direct speech. A big man in his early forties, he stood two inches taller than six feet and was the only man Matt had ever met who looked better with a mustache.

"You don't have to be polite to me, Matt."

"Yeah? Well, I feel crummy. I've worked my guts out punching my ticket for college ball, and in one lousy scrimmage I lost it all. It wasn't an accident, either. They meant to get me, and they did."

"It's too early to tell you not to look back, Matt. But you still have a year before you start college. That's time for your knee to heal and for you to get back in shape."

"In shape for what? No coach can afford to take a walk-on with an injured knee. There's no guarantee it won't happen again."

"There's no guaranteeing much of anything in this life, Matt. Sometimes you just have to punt. At least the doctor says your leg will heal." Bishop Adams paused a long moment. "I didn't come to preach at you. You'll get enough of that, even

10

without me. I just wanted you to know that I'm thinking about you. The whole ward is thinking of you, praying for you."

"Well, they'll never be able to pray me back on the team." Tears filled Matt's eyes, and he turned away.

Bishop Adams knew Matt wouldn't want to see him cry. Matt had always tried to be a tough kid. The bishop stirred uncomfortably, then stood. He slipped his gift into the curled arm of the silent young man. "Remember, Matt, when one door closes, the Lord opens another." He walked quietly from the room.

Matt cried silently, mourning his lost dream and hating Beef Kowalski. He refused to see visitors, and there were a string of them. The coach came, and Cindi Thompson, the head cheerleader.

Matt spent a long, restless night. Finally, toward morning, he pulled on the light and opened the gift from Bishop Adams. Nearly seven years had passed since he'd handled such a box, but he knew immediately that it was a model plane. Matt had lost interest in planes after his dad died. He almost threw this one in the wastebasket, but the model was a finely proportioned Cessna 310, a twin-engine civilian model, the sort built by people serious about model planes.

In spite of himself, Matt began to put it together. He endured interruptions for daily visits by Dr. Jackson, changes of bandages, even meals. He refused to see any visitors. When Marie announced, "There's someone special to see you," he shook his head and didn't even ask who it was.

He reread the flying magazine, worked on the model, and refused to be interested in anything else. He allowed his mother to visit; the rest of the world he shut out.

2

"The bishop's ready for you, Brother Stratford," Brother Hollins said.

Inside, Bishop Adams stood and extended his hand across the desk. "Thanks for coming in, Tom."

"No problem, Bishop. The worst you could do is ask me to teach Sunday School, and I'm already doing that. What can I do for you?"

"I've got a special home-teaching assignment for you. Most of the time, we don't have enough widows to go around, so I find some real challenging less-active families for my high priests. But you get a genuine widow." He grinned at Tom.

"Sounds easy enough so far. Who is she?"

"Nancy Hansen."

"You mean the Dragon Lady?"

"You've only been in the ward a month, Tom."

"That's long enough to hear the stories, Bishop. She's pretty, less than forty, and her boys are nice. That's enough to interest all the single brethren. She's a businesswoman, smart as a whip, absolutely dedicated to the gospel. That scares most of them away. Me, I'm not looking. She's the best Gospel Doctrine teacher I ever had. Made me sorry to have to teach a class of my own. What's the problem?"

"It's her boy, Matt. The older one."

"What's wrong with him? Seems like a nice kid. A little quiet, maybe."

"That's because you're new, Tom. Three months ago he

12

was the life of the ward. He was a football star, an honor student. Most of the kids liked him. He was my priests quorum first assistant. Maybe he was a little self-involved. He had dreams of pro ball, and he might have made it."

"He uses a cane," Tom said. "I thought he was handi-capped."

"Football injury. He hurt his knee in practice just before school started. He's sure he's lost his chance at college ball, and he doesn't care about anything else. It's just possible the injury wasn't an accident. Matt isn't very patient with others' mistakes."

"Be a surprise if he wasn't sore over that, if it's true."

"I've been bishop a long time, Tom. When most kids fall apart, they follow a pattern. They get angry; they have trouble with the standards. Matt's just getting dead. He won't participate in anything, but he doesn't cause trouble for anybody, either. I'd feel happier if he did. At least I'd know he was still alive."

"What do you want me to do, Bishop?"

"His mother came to see me. He's shut everybody out. You'd expect some depression, Tom, but it's been three months, and Matt isn't getting any better. His dad was an Air Force pilot. He was killed six or seven years ago. Matt never talks about flying, but I can't help thinking there's something there. You're a pilot. Maybe you can reach him."

"How do you figure Sister Hansen is going to like having a home teacher who's a pilot? Looks as if it'd bring back a lot of memories."

"It might be good for her, Tom. I'm not sure Matt needs all the help in that family. Sister Hansen's always in charge. It might be her way of trying to guarantee her life." Bishop Adams arose. "There aren't any guarantees in this life. That's why I sell insurance — to help people live with disasters."

"There aren't any guarantees," Tom agreed slowly as he stood up. "Not about anything."

13

He sounded defeated, and a little bitter. Bishop Adams considered what he was asking of Tom, but he still felt comfortable about it. He stuck out a hand, and Brother Stratford shook it. "See what you can do."

The victory parade wound through the streets, honking and shouting in the chill November air. Cumberland Ridge had won the state's 4–A football championship. The long procession passed the Hansen home. A black-and-silver Mazda pickup, lights blinking for a left turn, waited while the parade passed under Matt's window.

Matt tried to ignore the revelry. He had nothing to celebrate. The better the team had done the more Matt had hurt. Coach Robbins had invited Matt to sit with the team during assemblies and on the bench during games. He had refused.

"I can't play, Coach. What's the use of pretending I'm on the team?" Matt demanded the first time Robbins asked. And the second, and the third. The coach quit asking.

Beef tried to talk to him several times, but Matt refused. He hadn't realized that they were enemies before his injury, but Beef had made his point. The team didn't need him. Matt's football days were over.

He had nothing to do with football in any way. Not even Cindi Thompson. Though she was a good friend, she was the head cheerleader, so she fell under his resolute attitude. He avoided her, even at church.

Beep! Beep! Beep! Matt tightened his mouth and concentrated on the model he was building, an Ag Cat crop-duster. It was the first model he'd attempted from scratch. His room overflowed with models. Matt's mother was surprised when he had returned to model building. Not long after Big Matt's death, Matt had taken all his fighter models and boxed them up. "Dad died in one of those planes," he'd said. "I don't want them around."

It was a fairly normal reaction, she'd thought, as she helped him take them to the Goodwill collection center. The total reversal of his love for flight seemed only an aftermath of his father's fiery desert crash.

She was busy trying to put her own life together. With a new baby and an eleven-year-old, she was more concerned with helping her boys grow up well despite the lack of a father's influence. Although she wasn't much of a football fan, she'd been pleased when Matt kept playing. It was a link with his father's memory.

Nancy Hansen had seen enough boys grow up without fathers to recognize the problems, but in the years just after Matt's death, she couldn't imagine marrying again. Matt had been dynamic, strong, exciting. They'd been part of a patriotic mission they both believed in. In the early years of her widowhood, she hadn't wanted a romantic replacement. As the years wore on, Nancy admitted that Matt had also been single-minded, goal-oriented, and somewhat selfish. She realized that she'd often been lonely.

"It's better to be lonely single than lonely married," she told Bishop Adams. "I can make my own decisions, plan my own life. That's an advantage I didn't have when I was married. The last thing I want is candlelight dinners. At my age, the dating game is ridiculous." She had gone her competent way, until her teenaged son's accident.

As Matt withdrew, she worried. He was pleasant to her, and no more that normally impatient with six-year-old John. His grades were respectable, although Dr. Samuels, his advanced math teacher, told her that Matt worked far below his actual capacity. He didn't associate with anyone or get involved with anything. He just withdrew into an artificial world of planes that really didn't fly. He refused to participate in family scripture reading or say family prayers. He continued to use his cane long after Dr. Jackson told her he shouldn't need it.

15

Beep! Beep! Beep! The last of the parade passed under Matt's window. The pickup turned into the driveway. Matt concentrated on his model. He didn't even hear the doorbell ring.

Matt ignored the knock on his door ten minutes later. The door opened, and Matt turned. He didn't recognize the middle-aged man standing in the doorway. The man's grey hair curled closely against his head. His full face was lined; a network of tiny wrinkles webbed his eyes. He wasn't as tall as Matt. Although his shoulders were beginning to round, he still gave the impression of strength.

"Hi, Matt. I'm Tom Stratford, your new home teacher. Your mom said you were up here working on planes."

"Yeah." Matt turned back to the plane, hoping that the man would take the hint. He didn't. He came into the room, ducking around the models hanging from the ceiling.

"You've got quite a bunch here. Ever fly any of them?"

"Nope," Matt said shortly.

"Why not?"

"I've put too much work into them to crash them up." He continued working on the Ag Cat.

Tom Stratford wandered around the room, looking at the models. He paused next to Matt's desk. "That Grumann Ag Cat's looking good!"

"What do you know about planes?"

Tom ignored the rudeness. "Oh, I've had a little to do with them, time to time."

"Did you ever fly fighters?"

"Nope, but I've sure seen a bunch of them. I grew up in Virginia Beach. I was about your age when I started working at a little country airport in New Jersey, pumping fuel and doing odd jobs for the FBO that had the contract there. I've flown a lot of those planes you've built."

In spite of himself, Matt was interested. "Do you still fly?"

16

"That's how I keep food on the table. I fly checks for the Federal Reserve."

"Oh, yeah?"

"I'm at Harrisburg International by 8:30 five nights a week. The courier service brings the checks by 8:45, and I take off for Philly at nine."

"You fly to Philadelphia every night?"

"Sure. Checks to Philly. Then to Buffalo for medical stuff. I deliver that to Pottstown, then fly home to Harrisburg. Sometimes I'm rerouted."

Matt continued working on the Ag Cat, but his hands moved more slowly.

"It's not real exciting," Tom continued, "but it beats the heck out of being chained to a desk eight hours a day."

"What do you fly?"

"A Cessna 310." Tom looked around the room. "Got one?"

Matt gestured toward his dresser, where the Cessna 310 stood, poised for takeoff.

Tom crossed the room, put on his glasses, and studied the twin-engine model. "You've done a good job on it."

"Thanks," Matt mumbled. He stopped working on the crop duster.

"How come you specialize in civilian aircraft?" Tom asked "Most guys go for military ones."

"I don't like them. They kill people."

"I've always wanted to be a military pilot myself, but I never could pass the physical. Been in glasses since I was a kid. Well, there's no glory in flying a 310, but, like I said, it beats being chained to a desk."

"The pay's got to be good."

"Actually, it's not. Airline pilots make a bundle, but outside that, there're too many guys like me wanting to fly. We work for peanuts just to keep our certificates up to date."

"If there's no money in it, why do you fly?"

"It's the only thing that feels right. I've tried other things; couldn't stand them. Freedom's worth quite a bit to me. No one's looking over my shoulder during the night. I hardly ever see my boss. I pick up my paycheck while I'm waiting for my load in Pottstown."

Matt had given up all pretense of working on the model. This was the longest conversation he'd had with anyone since he came home from the hospital.

Tom looked around the room, then moved to the door. He paused, hand on the door frame. "You want to fly with me Friday night?"

"What do you want from me?" Matt demanded.

Tom shrugged. "A little company maybe. Thought you might like to come along."

"I don't want anybody taking care of me. I can take care of myself."

"Who says I'm trying to take care of you?"

"That's what home teachers're supposed to do."

"It's not my job to take care of you, Matt. That's your job, yours and God's."

"It doesn't look like God did such a great job. I did all the right things. And here I am, crippled." He glared at the cane propped against his desk.

"Don't see that it matters. You won't do much walking in the sky."

In spite of himself, Matt grinned.

"Look, Matt. I'm not trying to force you to fly. But I think you've got flying in your blood as bad as I do. If you want to do it, here's your chance."

"What'll your boss say?"

"We'll sign you on as a cargo handler." Tom smiled. "No pay, though."

"Mom won't let me. We never fly, even when we go to California to see my grandparents."

18

"You let me talk to your mother. If she says it's okay, do you want to go?"

"Sure. But she won't."

"I'll go ask her. Pick you up Friday about 8:15."

Tom walked down the stairs, and Matt returned to the Ag Cat. Brother Stratford sure was confident that he could deal with Matt's mom. Maybe Brother Stratford could bring her around. He did a good job on me, Matt decided.

Downstairs, Tom rescued his teenaged home-teaching companion from the six-year-old wrestler. "Is it okay if I take Matt with me on my job Friday night? We'll be late, maybe 2:30."

"Brother Stratford, if you can interest Matt in going with you anywhere, I'll be grateful." Matt's mother smiled. "What do you do?"

"I'm a pilot. I fly checks for the Federal Reserve."

Nancy Hansen's mouth tightened. She started to object, but Tom interrupted. "Look, when Bishop Adams gave me your family, he filled me in. I know how you feel."

"Nobody knows how I feel. I don't want another pilot in this family."

"You're apt to get one anyway," Tom replied.

"Not Matt. When his father was killed, Matt hated planes."

"He may have before. But when he lost his chance at football, what did he go back to? Planes."

"It's a long way from building models to actually flying. I'd be surprised if he'd go."

"He'll be surprised if you let him," Tom said, grinning.

"Oh, all right! Take him with you Friday. Maybe it'll do some good."

"Sister Hansen, when he's in the air, he won't need that cane."

3

"STATE CHAMPS," THE SIGNBOARD OUTSIDE THE high school announced. Jubilant signs festooned the corridors. Even the restroom walls were crowded with congratulatory posters. Matt found it impossible to ignore the colorful displays.

Since his return to school, he'd spent his PE periods alone in the library. Physical therapy had done little to eliminate his limp. The cane had become a shield of sorts.

Matt was leafing through a book on flight instruction when he saw Coach Robbins come into the room. His first impulse was to leave, but the cane slipped to the floor. Before he could retrieve it, Coach Robbins stood beside him. "Hansen, it's time we had a talk."

"Sure, Coach," Matt said, with a desperate show of disinterest.

Coach Robbins sat down. He brushed back his thinning hair and cleared his throat. Matt realized that the coach was nervous. "You should have been with us when we won the championship, Matt."

"Yeah," Matt said unhelpfully.

Coach Robbins hesitated. Matt stared at him, his fingers holding his place in the book.

The coach struggled to find the right words. He looked at Matt's advanced mathematics book resting on the table. "Math's like football, Matt. Your job is to find the right strategy for solving a problem. Sometimes we make mistakes, bad ones.

You can always toss away paper, but you can't do that with people."

He stopped. Matt said nothing.

"In football you've got eleven variables, not counting the other team. They're all motivated differently, sometimes inconsistently, often in areas a coach doesn't know about." He paused, then forged ahead. "Maybe you think I should have known, but I had no idea that you and Kowalski had it in for each other."

Matt finally responded, "It wasn't me. I didn't have anything against him. He said the team didn't need me, and it looks like he was right."

The coach looked at the cane. "Nobody's indispensable, Matt. We're all part of something. It's been a great team this year. It would have been even stronger with you on it, but that's not the point I wanted to make."

"What's the point, Coach? The season's over."

"I don't think Kowalski intended to hurt you as bad as he did. It's hard for him to live with, seeing you every day with that cane."

"It's not easy for me, Coach." Matt opened his book. "I don't want to talk about it anymore." He began to read.

Coach Robbins yielded to Matt's stubbornness. He clapped his former halfback on the shoulder. "Well, some of us see the problems, Matt. Others look for solutions." He was gone before Matt could respond.

Matt's brooding silence was broken by the loudspeaker. "Officer Benson and Rascal will patrol after lunch." Matt thought it funny that the principal always announced drug searches in advance. If anybody was worried about the drug dog's patrol, he had plenty of time to clean out his locker.

Drug problems had increased after the Cuban boat people were processed at Fort Indiantown Gap. Some of them weren't really refugees but inmates from the Mariel prison. Central

21

Pennsylvania had become a major funnel for drugs coming up from Florida into the northeastern United States and Canada. The Marielitos had begun to control that traffic. Matt didn't take any interest in drugs, but he'd have to be blind not to see them around school.

"Hi, Matt. Can I sit down?"

Matt looked up into Cindi Thompson's green eyes. "Sitting's free."

The auburn-haired cheerleader took the chair across from him. Matt had avoided her since his operation, though they'd been good friends since they were the entire Merrie Miss–Blazer A class in Primary. Matt thought it ridiculous that Beef was jealous of him because of Cindi. He'd never even taken her out. Cindi seemed oblivious to Beef's interest. Matt didn't know how she really felt.

"I wanted to tell you I missed you yesterday. Everybody misses you. You just don't know. It's like I never see you anymore." Cindi paused. "Mutual's having a service project Saturday. Why don't you come?"

"What is it?"

"We're going to wash Sister Haskell's windows and paint her living room."

Sister Haskell was the eighty-seven-year-old unofficial ward grandmother. She kept the Primary nursery and brought home-made cookies every Sunday. Her strength had diminished, but she told everyone that, as long as she could lift a cookie sheet, her useful days weren't over. She really did need help. Matt couldn't refuse. "Sure."

"Great! Can you pick me up? Dad's taking the truck to Baltimore to pick up a project car from a junkyard down there. Mom's car's not running."

"Uh, yeah. I guess so." Since his surgery, Matt hadn't been driving much.

"Great! Bring your little brother."

22

"Why?"

Cindi laughed. "You know Sister Haskell. She's got to have somebody to feed. He'll be our decoy while we get the work done. She loves having someone to talk with. And one thing you have to say about John—he sure loves to talk."

"And eat."

The bell rang. Matt picked up his cane and tucked it under his arm. He tried hard not to limp as he walked from the library with Cindi. Her next class was just two doors from his.

They said good-bye at the door. Matt's eyes followed her into the classroom. He felt comfortable for the first time since he'd returned to school. He turned back into the hall and saw Beef Kowalski trudging toward him. Matt put his cane down and limped past the huge player, pretending he hadn't seen him. Beef was stopped frequently by students congratulating him on the team's championship. He didn't seem to see Matt, either.

The rest of the day was miserable. The whole school talked about the championship. Matt was glad when three o'clock finally came and he got on one of the buses lined up around the school's circular drive.

The rest of the week passed slowly. During supper Friday night, Matt's mother announced she had a new job. "Only temporary," she said.

"What now, Mom?" Matt asked. His mother didn't have a regular job. She wanted to be her own boss, and she enjoyed selling. She'd tried real estate, which was successful, but she'd eventually given it up because the majority of her work was on weekends. She refused Sunday appointments, and Saturday ones left the boys alone.

Then she'd tried Avon. Matt could remember helping her sort orders. She'd been a President's Club member within six months, but with so many women working, deliveries had to be made mostly in the evenings and on Saturdays, so she had quit her route. She'd tried Amway, then Herbalife. Matt didn't know why she bothered. He didn't think it was the money. If she was going to work, it would sure be nice if she'd get a job like other people.

"I'm in charge of the Santa-in-the-Mall."

"What's that?" John asked.

"Every year they have Santas in the malls. Kids go in and sit on his lap and tell him what they want for Christmas. They get their pictures taken. I'm in charge of four malls; here, and in Carlisle, Harrisburg, and York. I'll hire the Santas and the helpers and make sure everything runs smoothly."

Oh, great! Matt thought. This is going to be a mess. Why does Mom do these things? "Where'd you find this job?"

"The company called Bishop Adams. They like to hire Mormons. How'd you like to be a Santa Claus?"

"You mean in a red suit?" John asked. "Wow! That'd be awesome."

"That'd be stupid!"

"It might build your mission fund, Matt."

"No." Matt hadn't mentioned his mission since his surgery. Before the injury, it had been another place to get his ticket punched. Now he didn't even want to think about it.

The three turned back to their dinner. "You boys'd better hurry with the dishes if you're going with Brother Stratford, Matt."

"Why don't we get a dishwasher?"

"I have one. In fact, I have two," his mother replied. Matt and John did the dishes.

"I'll be glad when I'm big," John said. "Then I can help Mom lots."

"Yeah, you can take over for me." Matt didn't like housework. His dad had never done dishes, but when he'd tried that line on his mother, he'd gotten nowhere. She had simply said,

"A man ought to be able to cook and clean and take care of his own clothes. You won't always have a mother around."

"I'll have a wife."

"She may not be able to wait on a grown man," his mother had snapped. Matt had started to argue, but from somewhere back in his childhood he remembered his mother in bed for what seemed like a long time. He had decided to drop the subject.

John ran to answer the knock on the kitchen door. Matt looked at the clock. Tom Stratford was right on time.

"Hi, John. Your brother here?"

"We just got done with the dishes. He can go now."

"Well, good for you guys! With two big kids, your mom has lots of help with the work."

John grinned with pride.

Tom wiped his feet on the mat inside the door. "It's wet out there."

Matt's heart sunk. "Does that mean we can't fly?"

"You ever heard the courier pilot's motto: 'Why get a weather report? We fly anyway.' The stuff we haul can't wait. We'll fly on instruments. Ready to go?"

Matt limped to the cellar door and pulled his coat from the hook inside. Tom waved "hi and bye" to Matt's mom.

"Be careful," she said as they left. "Come on, John, let's make popcorn."

Matt climbed into Tom's pickup. He winced as he folded his leg into the small space. Tom looked at him from the corner of his eye. They took the road to the turnpike. Tom reached out the window and slipped the ticket from the machine. They drove across the Susquehanna River to Exit 19, paid the waiting attendant, and took Highway 283 to the Middletown exit. Tom parked his truck behind one of the World War II-era buildings. He grabbed his briefcase, and Matt picked up his cane.

"Leave it, if you can, Matt. It'll just be in the way."

"Sure." He tossed the cane into the cab and shut the door. They walked through the shadows to a locked gate. Tom punched the buttons, and the lock snapped open. Matt limped as they hurried past the rows of single- and twin-engine planes. Tom stopped before a twin with pods on the wing tips.

"This is it," he announced as he opened the cargo door behind the wing and put his briefcase behind the right seat. He reached over on his tiptoes and pulled the gustlock out of the control column for the left seat, then led Matt through the ground check. "Safety's got to be our first concern. If your car quits, you pull off the road. If your plane quits, you fall out of the sky."

Flashlight in hand, Tom showed Matt how to pull the oil dipsticks. "We've got gauges inside that tell us how we are on oil and fuel, and I always make sure they're right by checking before I fly." When they finished the preflight procedures, Matt pulled the chocks blocking the wheels.

"Climb into the pilot's seat on the left," Tom said.

Matt looked at Tom with surprise.

"Don't worry," Tom reassured him. "I'm a certified flight instructor. I'm used to flying from the right seat."

Matt walked up the right wing and opened the door. He clambered across the seat and sat down. Dozens of dials and gauges stared him in the face. Tom showed him how to adjust his seat and put on the seatbelt. Switch by switch, he took Matt through the instrument checks. He switched on the ignitions, starting first one engine, then the other.

"Let's taxi over and pick up our load from the ground courier. Put your feet on the pedals. They control the tail and brakes. The steering column controls the ailerons and elevators. Down here, between us, are the throttles."

Tom edged both throttles forward, and the plane eased from its parking place. "Keep your feet on the pedals, but let me do the work."

26

Matt felt the pedals move as Tom taxied the plane to another building. Tom killed the engines and shut off the gauges. Only the marker lights remained active. He showed Matt how to insert the gustlock and set the brakes. They climbed down.

A van appeared out of the darkness. It backed up to the Cessna's cargo door. The driver, a tall man about retirement age, stepped out. Matt helped Tom and the driver load parcels into the compartment behind the seats. They put several smaller satchel-like packages into the nose compartment. "You've got to balance the load," Tom explained as the courier waved good-bye and drove away.

Once in the 310, Tom flipped on the radios. Ground control gave him clearance to taxi to the edge of the runway. "Stand on the brakes. That's it! Now, move each throttle, one at a time, to 1800 RPM twice, then to 2300, and back to 1000. That gets the oil where we need it."

Matt followed Tom's instructions, first with the left engine, then with the right. The craft rocked, eager to climb into the night sky.

Tom radioed the tower: "Flying Dutchman 2407, ready for takeoff for Philadelphia."

"Wait for the 727 coming in," the tower replied. Matt saw landing lights dropping down to the runway to his left. The aircraft hurtled past them, wheels just touching the ground. Matt could hear the scream of its jets over the Cessna's engines.

The radio came alive. "Flying Dutchman 2407, you're cleared for takeoff."

Tom eased off the brakes and pushed the throttles forward. The RPMs climbed on the two gauges. Matt felt the pedals move as Tom turned onto the runway.

"Put your hands on the throttles, but let me do the pushing," Tom instructed.

Matt put the heel of his right hand on the red knobs. Tom covered Matt's hand with his and pushed slowly but steadily.

27

"Watch our speed. We'll need a minimum of ninety-four knots for takeoff."

The 310 gathered speed as it straddled the runway's marker lights. "This is a good, long runway," Tom said. "Now Pottstown's short; we have to really rev our engines there before we release the brakes."

The airspeed indicator climbed past eighty knots, and Tom pulled back on the column. Matt felt the nose of the plane lift. The front wheel was off the ground. The indicator climbed past ninety-four knots. The column came back toward Matt's chest as the 310 lifted into the darkened sky.

Tom showed Matt how to bring up the landing gear and shut off the landing lights. "Twenty minutes to Philly. I hope you can fly with me again. You'll get some hours in."

"I thought I was just going along for the ride."

"You'd just as well learn to fly. It's free, which is a good price for most anything."

Matt grinned. He looked out on the night sky and saw a whole new world out there.

4

It was a world of confusion. Tom brought the plane to 5,000 feet, signed off with air traffic control at Harrisburg, and set his radio frequency for Philadelphia. He thumbed the mike. "Flying Dutchman 2407, with you at five thousand feet at Bucks Intersection with Information Zulu."

"Roger, Flying Dutchman 2407," a voice replied.

"There're a couple of differences between driving a car and flying a plane," Tom explained. "When you drive, you don't have to worry about up and down. You drive in only two dimensions, but you fly in three."

Tom pointed to the instrument panel. "There are a lot more instruments to pay attention to. The most important ones are right in front of you. Others are over here on your right. Check the main dials, one at a time, then glance over at these. Once you're familiar with the settings, it's easier. And you should be scanning the sky for other planes, like that one on your left."

Alarmed, Matt looked quickly. Far below in the distance he saw his neighbor's winking navigation lights.

Tom continued, "If there'd been a real problem, Philly would've warned us. Still, it's your responsibility to check for yourself. I knew a case one time when a controller completely missed a plane on his screen. The two planes were within five hundred feet of each other before he woke up. I always look."

"When you drove to the airport, you kept looking around."

Tom laughed. "Yeah, pilots have a reputation for being

rotten drivers. Our cockpit habits stay with us when we're just driving across town. My wife used to make me let her drive."

"You've got a family?"

"Not anymore," Tom said brusquely and busied himself with Philadelphia Tower.

Matt had become expert at shutting out people lately. He recognized the technique. Tom continued talking with the tower, getting permission to land.

"Keep your feet on the pedals and your hand on the column, Matt. We're going down."

Tom landed the Cessna 310, taxied to the freight area, and shut off the plane. They unloaded the cargo into a waiting van. When they returned to the plane, Matt said, "Wouldn't it make more sense to fly to Buffalo first, then go to Pottstown, then to Philly; or is the Buffalo shipment too heavy?"

"It's not the weight; it's the timing. We're flying checks for the Federal Reserve. Every minute the banks are paying interest. Can you imagine what the interest is on $80 million bucks for three hours at prime rate?"

Matt thought for less than a minute. "Yeah, at ten percent that's $2,700."

"You're pretty good at math, aren't you?"

"Sure. I like math — it's easy. You can count on it. Now history, that's something else!"

"Well, say it takes about forty extra gallons of fuel to fly the route we do. Then there's my salary and the use of the plane. Maybe flying to Buffalo by way of Philadelphia costs $200 more, but it saves the bank $2,700 in interest. So they pay darned well. Still, the boss would like to pick up a load to Buffalo."

Stars burned in the cold night sky as they flew above the clouds. Matt's leg began to ache. He rubbed it, then returned his hand to the controls.

Tom spoke, "Since we're still flying under instrument flight rules, we can't practice any maneuvers tonight. Maybe it'll be clear next Friday. I cleared it with your mom."

"How'd you manage that?"

"Oh, your mom's a pretty reasonable lady. Just a little strong-minded; nothing the matter with that."

Friday nights were school activities, Matt thought. On the other hand, when was the last time he'd done anything at school? Not since his surgery. Compared with a chance to fly, it was an easy choice. "Next Friday," Matt agreed.

Tom keyed his radio. "Flying Dutchman 2407, at eight thousand feet, ready to descend."

"Roger Flying Dutchman, clear to descend to four thousand feet. Watch for icing at six thousand."

"We're going through that ice as quickly as we can. You'd better let me take the controls." Tom turned on the wing lights, illuminating both wings. He took the 310 smoothly through the ice.

Matt watched ice form on the wings. "What about that ice?"

"The wing's leading edge is rubber. It's inflatable. Push the de-icer switch there by your left hand, Matt."

He hit the switch. The ice cracked and began breaking away as the craft cut through the air. "Switch off the wing lights," Tom said.

The plane dropped to four thousand feet. Tom got landing clearance, then eased back on the throttles, slowing the 310. "We're approaching the airport now. This is the base leg, so we'll go to half flaps and drop to 120 knots."

Below them, Buffalo spread its welcome mat of colored lights. Matt found the rotating green and white beacon off to their left.

"Flying Dutchman 2407, turn on heading twenty-four," the tower interrupted. "You should have the runway in sight."

Matt saw the runway dead ahead of them. "Roger," Tom replied.

31

"Proceed to land."

The pilot pushed the flaps button all the way. Matt felt the plane rise slightly with the extra lift from the flaps. Tom pulled back on the throttle, slowing the craft even more. His finger flicked the landing gear lever, and Matt felt the craft buck slightly as the wheels dropped and locked into position.

Tom landed the Cessna smoothly, picked up ground control on the radio, and followed its guidance to Taxiway Bravo. The 310 turned right and slipped around the cargo complex. Tom taxied to the end near the fence at the west edge of the cargo area, then turned the craft once more and shut off the engines.

They climbed out onto the wing, walked to the trailing edge, down the foot holds, and dropped to the ground. A light, icy rain needled them as they walked to the warehouse. A dolly loaded with boxes waited inside. "Good," Tom said, "he's already been here."

"What's in those boxes?"

"Medical tests, blood, stuff like that, for a lab in Pottstown." Tom paused, his hand on the dolly. "Look, we've got a few minutes. Come meet Donald Morrison, an old fishing buddy of mine."

They went down a hall into another room. Morrison was leaning back in a swivel chair, feet propped on the desk. His mustache drooped, and red hair bristled under a British driving cap, hiding his ears and collar. He wore jeans and a denim jacket. A pair of wide red suspenders crossed his yellow shirt. Matt placed his age somewhere in the late thirties.

"Hello, Stratford," he said. His smooth voice had a slight British accent.

"Hi, Morrison. Want you to meet a friend of mine, Matt Hansen. He's handling cargo for me tonight."

Morrison scraped one boot off the table, then the other.

32

He stuck out a large hand. "Any friend of Stratford's, and so on."

"Morrison's from England, but he lives in Toronto now. We flew for a commuter airline down in Florida a few years back."

"I stuck with them till they went under," Morrison added. "Then I did a spell of corporate flying. Taking these executive dudes around to their meetings and golf dates. Bunch of garbage," he said angrily. "They treated me as if I was a piece of furniture."

"What did you do before you came to Harrisburg, Tom?" Matt asked.

"Flying Dutchman had me in Philly before they transferred me to Harrisburg. I did some crop dusting in Arizona and filled a stint in the Texas oil fields, too.

"It's been a few years," Morrison said. "Now we're both flying freight. When are we going fishing again, Stratford?"

"Have to wait for spring, I guess."

"Get some time off, and we'll head down south."

"No such luck. We're short two pilots right now. No time off for anybody."

"That's the trouble with these rinky-dink freight outfits, Stratford. No bennies. But there's money to be made flying freight."

"Not in any company I ever flew for."

"It all depends on what you're hauling," Morrison returned. "You heard about the guy who ditched his DC-3 on a bulldozed mountaintop road in Tennessee. Can you imagine what kind of money he was making to just walk off and leave his plane? That's big bucks!"

"He must have been a heck of a pilot to put a DC-3 down there and walk away," Tom agreed. "Still, I wouldn't want that kind of job on my conscience."

"Oh, I don't know," Morrison replied. "Somebody's selling,

somebody's buying. You're just hauling freight. You don't know what's in those packages you haul. You're down there on the Marielito Corridor. Somebody puts an unauthorized package in your load, and bam!—you're a drug runner."

"I'd be innocent because I wouldn't know anything about it."

"Tell that one to the task force."

"Well, it's not likely I'll ever have to worry about it. What I'd better worry about is snow. Pottstown's an unregulated airport. If this rain changes to snow, we'll have a tough time. Come on, Matt, let's go."

As the two went through the warm-up procedure, Tom said, "I've flown more than twelve thousand hours, and I've never carried an illegal load. Don't let Morrison fool you. That's dangerous. A guy who'd run drugs will steal sheep."

"What's stealing sheep got to do with it?"

"That's an old Western expression. Means he'd do anything." Tom paused, "You ever seen anybody with an overdose?"

"Nope."

"I have. Somebody who'll make money from that kind of misery isn't anyone I want for a business partner. Especially if he figures I'm getting to know too much about his business. It's awful easy to sabotage a plane."

"Do many pilots run drugs?"

"It's so easy. You don't have to do anything. Just look the other way, cooperate a little. It seems so simple, but once you're in, there's no going back. The law wants you, and the people you work for won't let you out. You may be well paid, but you're still a slave. You've sold your integrity, you might say. I don't know about Morrison; I hope he's just talking."

"Are you guys good friends?"

"You know how it is. We worked together. We rented a plane a few times and went fishing in Canada. By the time the commuter airline folded, we were on separate paths. Hadn't seen him in years."

"He seems kind of mad at everybody."

"Lots of people like that around. Sometimes they even have a reason to be mad, but what does it get them? 'If you can change something, do it. If you can't, don't bellyache,' my dad used to say. Well, let's get this plane off the ground."

Tom showed Matt how to maneuver the plane around the building. They crossed the runway, then turned left, following two other aircraft to the far end of the strip. One by one, the planes received takeoff clearance. Matt lined up the 310 just ahead of the runway's hashmarks.

"There's a crosswind, Matt, so push your right pedal enough to keep the plane straight down the middle of the runway. Straddle the lights. As you gain speed, you'll find you can relax that pedal. It's a matter of coordination."

Tom helped him push the throttles smoothly forward. Matt carefully adjusted his pressure on the pedals. The craft gained speed, holding dead center down the runway.

"Eighty knots, Matt. Lighten the nose!"

Matt pulled back on the column with his left hand. His right hand continued to push the throttles forward. The craft tilted upward. Matt pulled the column back, and the city lights fell below the nose.

During the flight, Tom managed the radio, interspersing his navigation work with explanations about what he was doing. "I know this all sounds confusing. It's a lot to learn in one night. But you're doing good."

Matt nodded, staring out at the night sky.

"The easiest way to find Pottstown airport is to watch for the towers at the Limerick Power Plant. There's the beacon. Let's go in."

"Are we landing in the dark?"

"No. My radio's set on the airport's frequency. When I

depress the talk button on my mike three times, the runway lights come on.

"Hit the landing lights, Matt." They were on full flaps, landing gear down, when they crossed the road. They cleared the fence by what seemed to Matt scant inches, then touched down at the end of the runway.

The pilot pulled the RPMs back to idling speed and stood on the brakes. "This is a short runway," he said calmly as the craft shuddered to a halt. Tom stood on the left brake and revved the right engine. The Cessna neatly spun on its axis. They lumbered back up the runway to a taxiway leading to a darkened building and a waiting van with parking lights on.

By the time they'd shut down the plane and climbed out, the van had backed up to the right side of the 310, and the driver was opening his doors. They emptied the van's load onto the pavement, then unloaded the plane's shipment of medical materials into the van.

"You mind loading this stuff, Tom?" the driver said. "I've got a date."

"Go ahead. Matt and I can handle it."

Matt hustled boxes, although his leg began to really hurt. While he stopped to massage his knee, Tom loaded the last boxes. Within a few minutes they were back in the plane. Tom keyed his mike and announced their flight. "That's just in case someone else is coming in and I didn't see him." They taxied to the end of the runway. "I'll take this one alone," Tom said.

He stood on the brakes and pushed the throttles smoothly and rapidly. The craft strained against the brakes. When he lifted his feet off, the eager plane shot forward. It lifted off the ground with yards to spare.

Twenty minutes later, they were under tower control and landing at Harrisburg. Tom taxied the plane back to its parking place. They killed the engines and the controls, inserted the gustlock, and climbed out. Matt reset the chocks under the

36

wheels, and Tom secured the tiedowns. "Be embarrassing to have a plane get loose. Other owners don't like it when a loose plane bounces in among theirs. I knew a case—"

"You know a lot of cases," Matt said, grinning.

"You bet! 'I knew a case,' and 'it came to pass.' Let's go home."

5
_____

Saturday morning dawned clear and cold. Matt's mother woke him at 7:30. He turned over and groaned.

Dodging the hanging models, he padded downstairs, leaning on his cane. John and his mom were eating scrambled eggs and toast. "I kept your eggs warm," she said as he looked into the fridge. "Eat something, slug-a-bed."

"I'm not hungry," Matt replied, as he sat down with a glass of juice.

"How was your trip?"

"Great! Brother Stratford's teaching me to fly."

"Awesome!" John exclaimed. "Will he teach me?"

"Of course not. You're too young."

"I wanna fly! I wanna fly!" John beat a tatoo on the table with his fork.

"Stop that!" his mother commanded from the sink.

John continued banging on the table. Matt snatched the fork away. "Cool it!"

"You're not the boss of me!"

"Shut up, or I'll flush you down the toilet!"

"Matt!"

He turned to his mother. "I don't know why you let John get away with so much garbage." He took his cane from its place near the fridge and mounted the stairs to his room. His mother called after him, but he ignored her.

He flopped down at his desk and checked the stick-and-paper Ag Cat. The phone rang, but he ignored his extension

38

and began dressing. Since his accident, fewer and fewer people called him.

"Matt! Matt! The phone's for you."

Matt threw down his pajama top and picked up the bedside phone.

"Hi Matt, are you going to help us paint at Sister Haskell's today?"

Matt groaned. He'd forgotten all about the project. He poised like a tight-rope walker, not sure which way he should lean. Well, why not? He could stand the other kids for a few hours, and he *had* promised Cindi.

"Still need me to pick you up?"

"Thanks, I've got a ride. Don't forget our decoy."

"Heck, I forgot to ask Mom. But I don't think she'll care."

"See you soon."

Matt's mood lightened as he thought of Cindi. She was fourth in a family of six kids. She was slightly built, and fairly tall. Although she wasn't really pretty, she was so alive that people thought she was. Her father had a one-man body-and-fender shop, and her mother had a home daycare center. Cindi helped her mother with the children a lot. Maybe that was why she got along with John. She'd had lots of experience.

He'd better get his mother alone to ask her whether John could go. He heard her moving around in the bathroom. "Mom," he called from the hall.

Nancy stuck her head out the bathroom door. "I'm just scrubbing the tub. Come on in."

Matt perched against the vanity. "That was Cindi. We've got a service project at Sister Haskell's. Cindi wants me to bring John to talk to Sister Haskell while we work. D'you care?"

Matt's mother looked surprised, then thoughtful. "No, he could go. Get him to make his bed and put his dirty clothes in the hamper. Yours, too, Matt. Your room looks like a snake-pit." She turned back to the tub.

Matt realized that she had quietly taken over most of his chores. He hadn't thought about anything but his leg and later his models in a long time. "Here, Mom, if you'll finish the tub, I can do the sink and toilet while John's getting dressed." He didn't notice his mother's second look of surprise as she gave the tub a final rinse and went to call John to his room.

"I've got to be at the mall by one," she said as she gave Matt the keys.

A short time later, John was bouncing on the seat, excited to be going with Matt. "Sister Haskell's neat! She always talks to me."

Matt pulled into Sister Haskell's drive just as the bishop arrived with the rest of the young men. They piled from the bishop's van, full of jokes and energy. Matt reached into the car for his cane. His head had begun aching, and his leg hurt. Where was Cindi?

The five girls didn't appear until the young men were gathered in Sister Haskell's kitchen. Matt drew back into the corner as the bishop and Sister Miller, the Young Women's President, assigned chores.

For crying out loud, thought Matt. What did I get myself into? I can't climb a ladder and paint up high, and I can't kneel down to paint baseboards either. He was turning toward the door when Cindi saw him. She came across the room. "Matt," she said quietly, "come wash windows with me."

"Why?"

"I can do the outsides, but I need somebody to hold up the inside windows while we switch the storms. If you'll do that, we can get them done an awful lot faster."

Matt thought about it. She really did need someone to lift the big old-fashioned double-hung windows. "Yeah. I can do that."

Matt's leg was killing him by the time he and Cindi finished the last window. "I've got to get the car back for Mom," he said as they rinsed their buckets at the sink. He picked up his cane and started for the door.

Cindi followed him to the car. "Does it still hurt a lot?"

"It's getting better."

"I'm glad. Sometimes I can hardly stand thinking about it. It was awful all fall, Matt, without you on the team."

"Well, Beef was there."

"What's he got to do with it?"

Matt realized that Cindi had no idea that she was the reason Beef Kowalski had nailed him. Well, one of the reasons anyway, Matt had to admit. He had made the lineman appear stupid.

"Oh, nothing," Matt shrugged. "I was just talking. Come on, John," he called as he got into the car.

"Matt," Cindi hesitated. "Take me to the fireside tomorrow night?"

"Sorry, Cindi," he said. "I can barely stand church. At least, we're all sitting down there."

He started the car and backed from the drive.

"Are you mad at Cindi?" John asked as Matt gunned the car.

"No."

"Then how come you're mad?"

Matt didn't know why. He felt hopeless. Not being in control was a foreign feeling, and it made him angry.

When the boys got home, Nancy was ready to leave. She stood in the hall, purse in hand, her folder of time cards tucked under her arm. "Wish me luck. I hope every parent who puts his child on Santa's knee buys a picture today. It's all overhead until then."

"What's overhead?" John asked.

"Matt can tell you." She started out the door. "And, Matt, make lunch."

John went into the family room and turned on the TV. Matt rummaged around in the kitchen, trying to find something more interesting than peanut butter sandwiches. As he worked, he thought about his family. His mother had her succession of businesses and her business associates. When she was home, she had paperwork to do, or she was studying for her Gospel Doctrine class. John watched TV endlessly. Matt wondered why their mother let him. Matt hadn't been allowed to. Of course, when he was John's age, his father had been alive. Sometimes he could hardly remember what it was like, being an ordinary family.

Why did his mother jump into one business after another? This Santa idea sounded crazy to him. How could she make any money after she paid all her expenses? It really wasn't as though they needed the money. What was she trying to do?

Matt put a dish of left-over macaroni and cheese in the microwave, and called John in from the TV. After they'd eaten and washed dishes, Matt climbed the stairs to his room. He decided to start his homework. He'd really let himself get behind. He was still working calculus problems when his mother came home at suppertime.

"It'll work out," she said at dinner. "I've had to let two helpers go, and one Santa, but I've already got a replacement for one of the helpers. And I saw Brother Stratford at the mall. He's going to be a Santa."

"But, Mom, he's a pilot."

"I'm not asking him to give up flying. He's going to be a Santa in the afternoons. He may not have any kids, but he's comfortable with them, and they like him. He tried it when my Saturday Santa went to dinner."

Matt did the supper dishes while John took his bath. He mounted the stairs to his room, thinking about Sunday. He didn't enjoy going to church anymore. He was surprised at how empty it seemed when he didn't talk with the other kids. Used to be, the teacher could hardly shut Matt up. Somehow, there never seemed to be anything to say now.

Why had Cindi asked him to the fireside? She usually went with a group of girls, or with her dad, the ward's Young Men's President. Did she feel sorry for him? Matt didn't need anybody's pity. He just needed his leg instead of the darned cane. He grabbed the cane with both hands and jerked it over his good knee. The cane splintered and broke. He threw the pieces out his door, and they clattered on the stairs. He slammed the door.

"Mom," John cried, "Matt threw these sticks at me. I wasn't bothering him, honest I wasn't."

"Why, that's Matt's cane. Why ever did he throw it down the stairs?"

"He threw it at me. And all I was doing was going upstairs."

Nancy looked up the stairway to Matt's closed door. "I don't think he was throwing it at you, John. He probably didn't even know you were there. I think he just broke it and threw it out his door."

She started up the stairs toward Matt's room.

"Matt doesn't like me, Mom."

"Right now, Matt doesn't like anybody." Nancy paused outside the closed door. "Come on, John. We'll leave Matt alone. Let's go read a story."

The next day, Matt sat quietly through Sunday School. He gave Cindi a short "Hi" in reply to her greeting, then took a chair on the back row. Cindi shrugged and sat down in front. During priesthood, Matt sat out in the foyer. He'd asked to be released as priests quorum first assistant. But since he'd been released, he had felt useless. First the team, then the priests. They could get along just fine without him. Well, let them.

Matt's family always sat down front for sacrament meeting, a practice that had started when John was a toddler. "How can a child get anything from a meeting when he can't even see who's talking?" Nancy often said.

He saw Brother Stratford on the back row and raised a

43

hand. Tom smiled and nodded but made no effort to talk to Matt after the meeting.

Disappointed, Matt went straight to the car and waited for his mom and John. "You want me to drive, Mom?" he asked when they finally reached the car.

"I can do it."

It was just one more sign that he wasn't needed. He threw his books in the back and climbed in.

"Brother Stratford's coming for dinner tonight, boys. John, you left the comics all over the living-room floor again. Make sure you pick them up."

"When's he coming, Mom?" John asked.

"Around five."

"Then I've got plenty of time."

"You do it as soon as we get home. I don't want to worry about it. I'm going to cook a roast and make some pies."

"Why's he coming, Mom? He's already been here this month," Matt asked.

"I invited him. It's the least I can do when he's willing to help me. And he's teaching you to fly. I'd think you'd be glad to see him."

"Sorry, Mom. I don't know what's the matter with me lately."

"I don't either, Matt, but it's getting tiresome." She swung the car into the driveway. John jumped out and ran around the side of the house. "John, come and pick up the papers," she commanded.

"But Mom, I want to feed Honeysuckle," John explained.

"Didn't you feed her before we went to church?"

John shook his head.

"Feed her right now. Then get yourself in the house and do what I asked you." She sighed. John forgot far too often to feed his dog when he was supposed to. She headed toward the front door. Matt limped up the steps behind her.

44

By late afternoon, the house smelled wonderful. The roast was browning, and the pies were out of the oven. A tablecloth covered the table, which was set with the good china.

"That looks pretty, Mom," John said as Nancy adjusted the centerpiece.

His mother smiled. Matt realized that she was pleased at the compliment. He'd been about to ask her who she was trying to impress. Sarcastic comments seemed to come naturally to him now. He was glad he hadn't said anything.

When Tom Stratford came in the door, he held a flat package under his arm. He handed it to Nancy. "Something for the house."

She unwrapped it immediately. Matt looked over her shoulder. It was a gold-framed print of a cold, grey marsh. A pair of wild geese flew into the rising sun.

Tom bit his lip. "You remember the old Tennessee Ernie Ford song, the one about the brother to the old wild goose?"

Nancy nodded.

"Thought you might."

Matt looked at his mother in puzzlement. She had tears in her eyes.

Tom continued, "The person who gave me this said all pilots are brothers to the old wild goose. I wanted you to have it."

Matt felt ill-at-ease. Why didn't she say something, anything? "Thanks, Tom," he blurted out. "It's neat."

Tom looked at Matt blankly for a minute. Then he shrugged out of his heavy sheepskin coat and reached into the pocket. "Here, Matt." He drew out a slender hardbound book. "I meant to give this to you Friday. It's your logbook."

He handed his coat to John. "Before you hang my coat for me, take a look in the pockets."

John reached in and pulled out a small box. "Awesome! A Lego plane. Thanks!"

Matt leafed through the book. Tom had already logged their flight last Friday. Tom held out another book, this one paperbound. "This is your flight-instruction manual. There's a lot of technical stuff you'll need for your written test. I knew a case . . . " He broke off, grinning at Matt.

Matt grinned back, and the mood changed.

"Come and sit," Nancy said. "We're ready to eat."

"Can I say the prayer, Mom?" John asked. "Can I?"

"Of course."

The meal was an unqualified success. Tom praised everything from the onion soup to Matt's green salad. He sighed when he saw the pies. "Now you can get a fair-to-middling roast in a good restaurant, but I sure miss homemade pies."

John spoke up, "My mom lets you have a little piece of both kinds."

Nancy smiled. "Brother Stratford can have two big pieces."

Tom took two. So did Matt.

Tom offered to wash dishes. "That way, the boys don't mind having company." He and Nancy worked together while the boys cleared the table and put things away.

"Brother Stratford," John asked, "are you going to marry my mother?"

Nancy blushed, but Tom laughed. "Why? Do you want a steady dishwasher?"

"Come on, John," Matt said, "time for bed."

"You're not the boss of me!"

"Oh yes, I am. Mom's busy." He picked John up, turned him upside down and carried him over to the stairs. "You'll have to walk. I can't carry you up there."

Matt's mom gave him a smile of appreciation.

Tom wrung out the dishcloth. "Thanks for dinner. I'd better head for home. I've got to hit the sack if I'm going to play Santa daytimes."

When John came back downstairs dressed for bed, Matt

46

grabbed him. "Hey, stupid, don't you know better than to ask questions like that? You embarrassed Mom."

"But I want to know. Mom, are you going to marry Brother Stratford?"

"Of course not, John. I'm not going to marry anybody. We're doing fine just the way we are."

Matt wondered, but he couldn't picture Tom as anything but a night pilot, a loner. Brother to the old wild goose. It fit.

"Oh, Matt," Nancy said, "Bishop Adams wants to talk to you Tuesday night."

Matt felt cold. The bishop was bound to want something, and he didn't have anything to give. "I'm not going."

He turned and pulled himself upstairs, wishing he hadn't broken his cane. His mother called after him, but he shut the door to his room.

6

Matt's AP math class checked homework answers against the letters and figures swiftly given in Dr. Samuel's dry voice. No other noise was heard in the classroom. Dr. Samuels didn't repeat himself. If you didn't hear him correctly the first time, you counted the answer wrong. Matt was pleased when Dr. Samuels finished. He'd gotten all the problems correct.

"Did anyone get a perfect score?" Dr. Samuels asked.

Matt and another student, Chico Cruz, raised their hands.

Dr. Samuels looked faintly pleased. He was a tall, slightly built man of indeterminate age. A former college professor, he had been teaching at Cumberland Ridge for six or seven years. Nobody knew much about him. His students didn't dislike him, but Matt had never met anyone who actively liked him, either.

Dr. Samuels believed every student could learn math. He used the controversial Saxon incremental method of teaching, frequently supplying extra books for his students. Cumberland Ridge qualified more AP students for college credit than any other high school in the state. Most of them were Dr. Samuels's students.

Dr. Samuels began his explanation of the next section. The class worked problems, occasionally asking for help. Dr. Samuels gave it in his neutral voice. He never embarrassed his students when they asked questions, but he seldom gave much praise, either. He treated advanced math as nonchalantly as most people treat driving a car. He expected everyone to do it. The bell rang and the students rose to leave.

"Mr. Cruz and Mr. Hansen, please remain after class."

The two young men stood before the teacher's desk. "I'd like both of you to enter the district advanced math competition. I'm prepared to tutor you. You have excellent chances of doing well." He gave another faint smile.

Chico smiled broadly. "Do you think I can do this advanced mathematics well?"

"Very well."

"Is it possible for me to get a scholarship, Dr. Samuels?" he asked.

"I think so, Mr. Cruz. You certainly have ability. Mr. Hansen, you have a great deal of ability, too. If you worked at anything approaching your capability, you could earn advanced degrees. It's a shame you've wasted so much of your time playing football."

Matt was shocked at Dr. Samuels's dismissal of what had been the focus of his life. "But football is my life. I want to play pro ball."

"What we want is often not what we actually get in life, Mr. Hansen. When I taught college, I saw ex-football players whose legs were ruined for life. Some of them had nothing else. You can use your brain when you're flat on your back. I suggest you take advantage of what really is a remarkable gift."

The two young men left the room, each deep in thought. At the lunchroom door, Chico paused. "I am having a little party Friday night. We eat, we rent a video. Would you like to come?"

"I'm sorry I can't." He realized it sounded like an excuse.

Chico's face fell. "That is all right," he said.

"No, really," Matt responded. "I'd like to. But I have this friend who's teaching me to fly. We fly every Friday night."

"You fly at night? Is that a good time to learn?" Chico didn't believe him.

"It's not the best time," Matt explained, "but my instructor's a freight pilot. He flies nights."

"I've never flown in a plane."

"My dad was a pilot, but I haven't flown since I was a kid. It's awesome." Matt's eyes sparkled, and for the first time since his surgery, he actually looked alive. He noticed other students looking at them. "Let's eat," he said.

Tuesday evening came too soon. Matt's mother was studying her Sunday School lesson. John talked about his friends at kindergarten. Matt stayed in his shell. He hadn't told his mother about the district math competition. He remained firm in his resolve not to go see the bishop. After supper he retreated to his room and shut the door. About 8 P.M. he heard a knock on the door. "Come in."

Matt was surprised to see Bishop Adams standing in the doorway.

"Mind if I sit down?" He perched on the edge of Matt's bed. There was a long silence. "You're the one, all right," Bishop Adams said finally.

"The one what?" Matt asked. He'd known the bishop wanted something.

"I've got a home teacher who needs a junior companion."

"Who?"

"Me."

Matt's mouth dropped open.

"Don't blame me," the bishop exclaimed. "My high priest group leader told me to find my own companion, bless his heart, so I've been fasting and praying. The Spirit keeps saying 'Matt Hansen.'"

"That's dumb."

"If you don't like it, you argue with him. I'm tired of doing it myself," he said with a wry smile.

Matt opened his mouth to say no, but "I'll think about it" came out.

"That's a good start," Bishop Adams agreed. "But it isn't enough."

"How come?"

"I fasted and prayed to get my answer. That's the least you can do. I wouldn't want you to take the job without doing your spiritual homework. Since I'm bishop, I only have two families, but they both need help."

"Bishop, I barely go to church."

"The Lord knows that."

The last thing I need is people with problems, thought Matt. I don't even know what to do about my own. A seminary scripture went through his mind. Something about finding yourself by losing yourself in the service of others. "All right," he decided.

The bishop looked surprised. "I'll have to interview you."

Matt had never had trouble passing an interview, but the bishop went farther than the handbook. "How's your temptation to gossip? These families have real problems, Matt. Nothing you hear or see can be mentioned in the ward."

"I never talk to anyone anymore."

"How are you on judging people?"

"I don't know."

"That's an honest answer, Matt. We're home teachers, not judges, so our job is just to love and help."

All Matt had done before was read a lesson or make phone calls. The bishop wanted something more from him.

Bishop Adams continued, "Sometimes things happen to us that make life mighty tough."

Matt found himself telling the bishop about his injury and his feelings for Beef Kowalski.

The bishop whistled. "Well, that does explain things. Your answer's not simple, Matt, but it's clear. You've got to forgive him."

Matt frowned. "Just like that? He hasn't repented."

"How do you know? Are you a mind reader?"

"He never said he was sorry."

"Did you ever give him a chance?"

"Of course not. I don't want anything to do with him."

"Well, that's better than wanting to beat his head in, but it's not enough. Corner him and tell him you're sorry."

"*I'm* sorry!"

"The initial offense may have been his, but the final offense is yours. He didn't mean to really hurt you. I bet he's suffering now."

"I don't see how. He got just what he wanted."

"He probably wanted to humble you a little, teach you a lesson. Being responsible for your condition must be tough on him."

"This is tough on me too, Bishop."

"I know it is, Matt, but you have someone to blame. Beef has no one to blame but himself. I don't know a worse feeling."

The bishop paused and picked up the 310 model. "You know, when you were in the hospital, I asked the Lord what to bring you to help you pass the time. He suggested a model plane. I don't know the first thing about airplanes, so I had a hard time choosing.

"First, I picked up an F-15 like your father flew, but I got my hands slapped, so to speak. It wasn't right for you. Three times I checked through the planes in that hobby store, and each time I put my hand on this one. I knew it was the right one."

"The plane Brother Stratford and I fly is a 310."

"There you are, then. How do you like flying?"

"It sure beats building models." He showed the bishop his log book and described the flight.

"Real life is always better than the substitutes, Matt, but it's harder." He stood up. "I'd better be going. You need to talk to that lineman. I'll call you."

Matt followed the bishop downstairs. He didn't even notice that he wasn't using the rail.

Matt didn't catch up with Kowalski until after lunch the next day. Beef seemed surprised, but he left his friends when Matt said, "I've got to talk to you."

They walked twenty feet down the hall and leaned against the tenth-grade lockers. Matt plunged into his speech, "Look, Kowalski, I'm sorry."

The lineman stared, a frown on his face.

Matt tried to explain, but it wasn't easy. The harder he tried, the more scrambled his thoughts became. "I know you didn't mean to ice me for good. It's all right."

The frown smoothed out. Crinkles appeared around Beef's eyes; a grin split his face. He began to laugh.

Matt turned on his heel and hurried down the hall. "Well, so much for that, Bishop," he said under his breath, slamming his fist into a locker. Fortunately, he missed hitting the handle and hurting his hand. Unfortunately, the hall monitor saw him, wrote up a white slip, and sent him to the principal's office. The principal gave Matt an hour of after-school detention.

"But I have to take the bus home," Matt tried to explain.

"I'm sorry. You'll have to wait for the activity bus at six."

Detention consisted of sitting in a classroom with a very bored Dr. Samuels, who kept himself busy correcting papers. Matt and the four others on detention were allowed to do nothing but sit quietly, watching the clock. They couldn't even do homework. Matt gazed out the window and thought about Friday. He relived the takeoffs, the moment when he left earth and mounted into the night sky.

Someone stirred, and Dr. Samuels looked up from his papers. The room grew quiet again. Dr. Samuels returned to his work.

Matt was back in the night sky when he heard Dr. Samuels stand and tap his papers lightly on the desk. "Detention is over."

Matt was the last one out the door. He turned left and nearly ran into Beef.

"Give you a lift home, Hansen?"

"Uh, sure. Thanks. The last thing I need is to wait another couple of hours for the activity bus."

"Right. I'm parked out front. Come on." He strode ahead, caught himself, and waited for Matt's slower gait.

"Does it hurt?"

"Not so much any more. It's just awkward."

They climbed into Beef's maroon 280-Z. "This is some car!" Matt exclaimed.

"Yeah. I just wish it was mine."

"Isn't it?"

"No way! Dad lets me drive the demos until they have their miles on them, then back they go. You never know what I might show up in next." Beef changed the subject, "I hear you're flying."

"Where'd you hear that?"

"Chico told me. He tutors me in math."

"He asked me to his party Friday."

"He needs some friends. His brothers are a mess, and he doesn't have any other family."

The two young men rode silently across town. Beef swung the low-built car into Matt's driveway and shut off the engine. "Look, Matt, I'm sorry I laughed when you were trying to talk to me."

"That's all right."

"No, it's not. When I tried to talk to you at the hospital,

54

you wouldn't even see me. I've been trying to get enough guts to apologize for hurting you, and here you came apologizing to me. It struck me funny. When I clipped you, I only meant to rough you up a little. I honestly didn't see Wilson."

"I thought you guys planned it."

"I figured you did when you quit the team. It wasn't the same without you."

"Well, life's tough."

"Sure, but I didn't need to make it tougher on you. I've always envied you."

"Envied me?"

"Yeah. You make math look so darned easy. Then there's Cindi. She won't give me the time of day. Every time I turned around, she was with you. I haven't seen you with her so much lately. If you guys broke up, maybe you could tell me how to get to first base with her."

"Cindi and I are just friends, Beef."

"Well, give me a break, then."

Matt laughed. "Well, if you want to get to first base with Cindi, you'll have to do two things."

"What are they?"

"You've got to come to church. She doesn't date anyone who doesn't."

"Your church?"

"Yep."

"Well, what else?"

"This one is the biggie."

"Yeah?"

"Don't ever try for second base."

"I wouldn't. Not with Cindi. She's special."

"If you got there, she wouldn't be special to you anymore." Matt couldn't believe it. He was beginning to sound like Bishop Adams!

"I don't know what my folks are going to say. We never

go to church except on Christmas or Easter. You'll have to help me."

"Me? How?"

"Well, I don't know anything about your services. Maybe I could sit with your family. You could kind of show me the ropes."

"Sure," Matt agreed.

"What time should I pick you up?"

"Oh, about twenty minutes to nine. Sunday School's first. Cindi's in our class. Then comes priesthood, then sacrament meeting. That's communion."

"What's priesthood?"

"All the men in the church have the priesthood. We meet in groups. You'll be in my group." Matt thought hard. He'd have to go with Beef. He could hardly sit in the foyer when he had a visitor. Oh, well, Cindi's dad was their advisor. That wouldn't be such a bad thing for Beef.

"I'll pick you up."

Matt sat on the porch steps as Beef drove away. There were no lights. Matt hated to go into the empty house. It always seemed cold when his mom wasn't home. He went to get John from Mrs. Bare's.

John clasped his hand tightly as they walked across the darkening yard. "I'm hungry," he said.

"Mrs. Bare said you had supper."

"I only ate a little bit. It was yucky!"

"Tell you what. Let's walk down to the store and get some donuts."

"It's too dark!"

"The street lights will be on soon. I can't leave you home alone, can I?"

"No!"

The fear in John's voice surprised Matt. He'd always thought

56

John had it easy. No worries, no problems. "Well, you'll have to go with me."

"Will you hold my hand?"

Matt bit back a sarcastic remark. His little brother held his hand tightly all the way to the store. Matt selected a half-dozen donuts at the bakery counter. On the way home, they ate them all. About midway, John let go of Matt's hand and walked alone. "Thanks, Matt."

"How come you're afraid to go out in the dark? There's nothing there that isn't there in the daytime."

"How come all the scary movies happen at night?"

Matt didn't have an answer. No wonder John raced home from the sitter's house. No wonder he always turned on the TV when his mother was gone and Matt was shut away in his room. The poor kid was really scared. "Hey, John, how'd you like to help me with my model when we get home?"

"Could I really? Gee, that would be awesome!"

They were in the middle of the project when their mother came home. It was going well, in spite of John's insistence that he knew more about model building than he really did. Several times Matt had to hold his temper as he adjusted to his new role of big brother teaching little brother.

"Matt? John?"

"Up here, Mom," Matt called.

Nancy came upstairs. "Looks like you two are having a good time," she said from the doorway.

"We are, Mom. Matt's a good brother after all."

For the first time in a long while, Matt felt the urge to laugh.

7

W<small>HEN</small> M<small>ATT</small> <small>CAME</small> <small>HOME</small> <small>FROM</small> <small>SCHOOL</small> Friday afternoon, he saw
Tom's pickup in the driveway. But when he walked into the
kitchen, no one was there. Matt found a note stuck to the fridge:
"Matt, keys under the seat of the truck. Pick up John and come
to the mall about seven. I'll take you and John to dinner. Your
mom will collect John. Tom." He went next door to get John.

John ran to greet him. "Hi, Matt! Where's Mom?"

"I don't know. Brother Stratford left his truck for us. He's
taking us to dinner before we fly. Mom'll pick you up at the
mall."

"Can we go to McDonald's?"

"We'll go wherever Brother Stratford wants to take us.
You'd better change your shirt. What've you been doing, making mud pies?"

"Nope, finger painting. Say, Matt, did you know that if you
mix orange and green and a little bit of purple, you get brown,
sort of?"

"That's what you got, all right. Go wash up. I wouldn't take
you to a dog fight in that shirt."

"All right. If I have to."

"You have to."

Less than half an hour later, Matt and John walked quickly
to the center of the mall. The fountain had been covered with
plywood and fake snow and decorated with Christmas trees.
Santa had his headquarters nearby. Cindi was there, dressed

in black slacks and a white blouse. A picket fence surrounded the booth, with a large throne-type chair at the back.

Matt had never seen a sadder Santa. Although he was well padded, the man was obviously tall and thin. His red nose needed no cosmetics. His eyes, under the fake bushy white brows, were watery. He managed a smile as a child was placed on his lap, but he was awkward, almost stiff, as he held him.

Four families waited. Cindi smiled as she talked with them, finding out each child's name, drawing smiles in return. As each one sat on Santa's lap, she coaxed a smile, stepping quickly to the camera to snap a picture. When the Polaroid coughed up the photos, Cindi mounted them in cardboard frames.

"Have you seen Brother Stratford?" Matt asked.

"He just went to change," Cindi replied as she prepared the camera for the next customer. "You're supposed to meet him here."

"How come he was working so late?"

"The guy that works Friday nights didn't show up, so your mom asked him to stay while she called Mr. Rawlins to see if he could come in. I don't know what she'll do if the regular Friday-night and Saturday Santa quits. Mr. Rawlins can only work four nights a week because of his health."

"How's Brother Stratford doing?"

"Hey, he's great, Matt! He sure knows how to talk to kids. I've gotten some really cute pictures."

"This guy doesn't look very good."

"He's real tense, and the kids can feel it. Then, too, he's thin, and a couple of older kids figured out he was padded."

"He looks like he's trying. Hey, Cindi, I talked with Beef this week."

Cindi's eyes brightened. "Did you really? That's great! He's been trying to get up the nerve to talk to you for months."

"How'd you know?"

59

"Just from watching him whenever you were around. He feels awful about your leg."

"That's what he said. We got it all straightened out. Tell me, do you like Beef?"

"Sure, I like him. I like just about everybody."

"He's a good guy. He's coming to church with me Sunday."

"You're kidding!"

John darted around the Christmas tree. "Here comes Brother Stratford!"

By the time Tom, Matt, and John had finished their meal at the Roy Rogers near the Santa booth, Matt's mother had arrived. She hurried into the restaurant.

"Sit down and grab a bite," Tom invited.

"I haven't a minute," Nancy replied.

"Sure you do. Save Cindi picking you up when you faint from hunger later on."

"Maybe you're right. I'll have a small chef's salad."

"I'll get it, Mom," Matt volunteered.

Tom shoved his chair back and stuck out his feet. "We'll be a little late tonight. I've been rerouted."

Nancy looked uncomfortable.

"Look," Tom added, "Matt can call you as soon as we know for sure. No top secret clearance on this job! We may not know what we're doing, but we can tell everybody." Tom grinned.

Nancy relaxed, "Oh, all right. Thanks for the salad, Tom."

"Hadn't we better be on our way, Tom?" Matt asked.

Tom looked at his watch. "Sure had. Thanks for the loan of your son."

On the way to the airport, Tom reviewed flight instructions with Matt. "You remember things real well. Tonight, I'll show you more about the radios."

They went through the preflight procedures and taxied the plane to meet the courier. "No checks for you tonight, Stratford.

One of the other pilots is going to Philly. You're empty to Buffalo."

Once inside the craft, Tom explained the radios, then Matt keyed the mike, "Flying Dutchman 2407, with Information Yankee, ready for taxi."

"There's a Convair ahead of you," ground control responded. They received clearance as the Convair moved onto the runway. "Flying Dutchman 2407, proceed to taxi."

Under Tom's direction, Matt maneuvered the plane toward the runway. The Convair in front hesitated briefly at the end of the runway and switched on its lights. It started rolling, engines whining. They watched it roar down the middle of the runway and lift into the sky.

The Cessna pulled up. The craft rocked gently as Matt stood on the brakes.

"Remember to rev each engine three times," Tom instructed. "Now, take the mike and say, 'Flying Dutchman 2407, ready for takeoff.' "

Matt's mouth went dry. Taking a plane off the ground in dreams was one thing; actually doing it was another. Matt keyed the mike, and the tower gave him permission. The 310 lumbered onto the runway, its landing lights rotating into position. The runway lights stretched into the night. Matt steadied the plane and looked at Tom.

"There's no wind tonight. Keep your rudder straight, and you'll be okay," Tom instructed. "Remember, at eighty knots you lighten the nose, and at ninety-four you pull back a little harder on the column, and we're off the ground. You won't have any trouble."

Matt nodded, his jaw clenched. He'd gone over the maneuvers frequently in his mind during the last week, but this was the real thing. It felt like opening play after kickoff, and he had the ball. He imagined running off the side of the runway, causing a mess, giving Tom another "I knew a case."

"Push the throttles," Tom said. "I won't be helping you."

Matt pushed, and the craft moved down the runway. His right hand continued pushing. Runway lights sped past. The 310 seemed to come alive as his feet lightly worked the pedals.

"Keep to the center," Tom warned quietly when the craft veered to the right. The Cessna centered on the runway as the airspeed indicator needle lifted farther from the peg.

Matt pulled back slightly on the column and felt the machine tilt. His hand continued easing the throttles forward. Matt felt the wheels leave the runway. The altimeter came to life. They were airborne.

"Bring up the landing gear and switch off the landing lights."

Matt flicked the switch and felt the wheels come into the plane. As they gained speed and altitude, the tower gave them a turn instruction, then released them to New York Central. Tom set the second radio for Buffalo.

When Matt reached eight thousand feet, Tom showed him how to level off and readjust his fuel mixtures and throttle settings for a steady 180 knots. Matt sighed and stretched his shoulders.

"Not bad, Matt. You'll make a pilot."

"Thanks, Tom." Matt was both pleased and relieved. "How'd you come to leave the truck at our house?"

"Your mom called me. She had to go to York. She was trying to juggle John, you, dinner, and four malls. Since I was going in anyway, I told her she could drop me at our mall on her way to York. When we got there, the regular Santa had left a note that he wasn't coming in. So I told her I'd cover until Harold Rawlins got there."

"He's not much of a Santa, is he?"

"I feel sorry for him, Matt. He's a long-time alcoholic who's really trying hard to stay dry. He probably won't make it, but he's trying so hard it hurts to watch. Your mom wants to give him all the help she can."

"Mom's always doing things like that. Everytime she gets into some new business, there's someone to help. She'd make more money if she stuck to business. I remember this one lady when Mom sold Herbalife. She called Mom every day and talked for hours. It was a waste of time; she never did make a good saleslady."

"Your mom told me about her. She was so shy, she could hardly talk to people when she started. Did you know she lost 103 pounds?"

"Boy, I'll bet that made a big difference in her life."

"Your mom knew that listening was the only thing she could do to help, so she did it, even when it cost her."

"It sure took a lot of time away from Mom's business though."

"It did. But then, I don't think your mom's trying to make money."

"Then what is she trying to do? She's always going into business."

"Seems to me she's trying to find out where she fits."

"What d'you mean?"

"I'm not sure I can explain it. Everybody has a place where they fit in. If they're not in it, things don't feel right. We find our place partly when we choose our work. You know, like a pilot, or a teacher, or a doctor, or a football player, or—"

"Or a mom," Matt interrupted.

"That's right. But your dad's not here. She's had a lot of years with just you kids, and she knows she's got years ahead of her. She's trying to fit who she is with where she is now. But if her only place is a mom, what'll she do when you kids are grown?"

"I never thought of it like that."

"I don't think your mom has, either. She's just looking. She understands the gospel; she has a strong testimony. I don't think she realizes what she's looking for, but she knows she hasn't found it. That's why she keeps trying something else."

"You sound like Bishop Adams. Have you ever been a bishop, Tom?"

"Nope. I was a branch president when I was a married student at Princeton, though. Don't suppose I was a very good one. That's when I was young and thought everything was simple."

"You went to Princeton?"

"Sure, why not? My dad had transferred from Virginia to Jersey. It was close."

"I thought you had to be really smart to go to Princeton."

"Thanks," Tom said drily.

"Oh, gosh, that's not what I meant. I'm sorry."

"No problem. I know what you mean. Princeton has an image, doesn't it? Well, now you know." Tom grinned.

"What'd you major in?"

"Math. I've got a master's. Thought I might teach. But I couldn't leave the planes alone. The only way I could get with the airlines was to have a good degree."

"Did you fly for an airline?"

"Four years on the West Coast," Tom replied.

"How come you didn't stay there?"

"Spent a long time in the hospital. They didn't hold my job for me."

Matt saw the wall come up. Tom leaned forward and keyed the mike. "Flying Dutchman 2407, requesting permission to land."

Matt looked down. He found the beacon easily. It still amazed him how the tower could bring them through the cloud cover and put them right in front of the runway.

Tom landed the plane smoothly. They parked the plane, shut off the controls, and climbed down the wing. Matt went for the dolly, and they loaded boxes and mailing envelopes. The medical supplies hadn't arrived.

"Let's check in on Morrison," Tom said. "There's his blue Aztec."

Tom led the way down the hall, but Morrison was nowhere around. "That's funny," Tom said. "Oh, well, let's go outside and wait for the courier."

"How's school?" he asked as they waited.

"Good." Matt told him about his math class and Dr. Samuels's invitation to the district math competition.

"Stewart Samuels? Long, tall guy, sort of grey all over?"

"That's him."

"I'll be darned."

"Do you know him?"

"Seen him a few times at the airport. He flies too. I didn't know he taught at Cumberland Ridge. You going to enter the competition?"

"Yeah, I am. Chico Cruz, he's this Cuban guy, and I. We'll need one more to make the team."

"I'd sure enjoy going to the competition with you. When is it?"

"Not until February. Let's see if Chico wants to ride with us too. Beef was telling me about him. He's got a couple of brothers, Marielitos, but the rest of his family's back in Cuba. Beef says his brothers are bad news."

"Beef? Isn't that the guy who laid you out?"

"Yeah. He gave me a ride home the other day."

"How'd that come about?"

"It was after he laughed at me when I apologized to him."

"Come on, Matt, give!"

Matt told Tom about his talk with the bishop. "Beef's coming to church with me Sunday. He really likes Cindi."

"That's great, Matt. You won't have to worry about Cindi — she's got her head on straight."

Tom pulled up his collar. "It's always windy in Buffalo," he said, "and generally cloudy. Has to do with the lakes. Here comes the rest of our load."

The courier stacked the boxes on the waiting dolly. Matt pushed it over the plane. They loaded the shipment, climbed the wing, and got in. Matt taxied the plane around the building. Ground control guided them to Runway 24. Tom reviewed takeoff instructions with Matt and said, "I'll be on the controls too."

If Tom was on the controls, his touch was so light that Matt couldn't feel it. Matt twisted the wheel slightly to the right and depressed the right pedal as he pushed the throttles forward. As the craft gained speed, Matt relaxed the ailerons and tail. He lifted the craft off the runway, pulled up the landing gear, and switched off the landing lights.

"Well done, Matt!"

Matt took the plane up toward their flying altitude. He felt warm with pride. He could fly. His feelings of self-congratulation lasted only a few seconds.

"Push the nose down!" Tom barked.

With a start, Matt realized that he was four hundred feet above his authorized altitude. He quickly pushed the wheel forward. As the plane began dropping, the tower demanded, "Flying Dutchman 2407, what is your altimeter reading?" Tom delayed his reply. "What is your altimeter reading?" the tower demanded again.

They were within the standard two hundred feet leeway allowed by FAA regulations when Tom gave their altitude.

Matt glanced nervously at the pilot. "I'm sorry, Tom. I should have paid closer attention."

"You never have time to dream, Matt. There's no time for doing anything but flying. That's why it's such hard work. You've got to watch your instruments all the time."

When they landed at Pottstown, the courier was waiting

66

for them. "It's good to see you, Tom," he said as they off-loaded the boxes.

"It's been a while. I'm based in Harrisburg now." Tom clapped the other man on the shoulder. "Come on, Matt, let's go get my check."

Tom led the way through the building and upstairs to Flying Dutchman's offices. A man in his late twenties sat at the second desk, working his way through a tall stack of papers.

"Vic," Tom said as they entered the room, "this is Matt Hansen. He's flying with me tonight."

Vic glanced up through a cloud of cigarette smoke.

"Hi, Matt. Hey, aren't you the Cumberland Ridge halfback who got injured and was out all season?"

"Yeah."

"Pleasure to meet you," Vic said as they shook hands. "I saw you play against Maryland last year. Great game! Tom, your check's in the slot."

"What's keeping you burning the midnight oil?"

Vic sighed, "The FAA. What else? They want me here whenever our planes are in the sky. I've got to coordinate everybody's flight loads. Don't be surprised if they ramp you sometime soon. Reminds me, Van Ryck wants you to go on to Teterboro."

"What for?"

"How would I know? He never tells me anything."

Tom turned to Matt. "I'll call your mom and tell her we'll be late."

"What's ramped?" Matt asked as they walked through the darkness to the waiting plane.

"The ramp's where we park the planes. Getting ramped means the FAA holds you there while they check you out. Sort of like being pulled over by the state police. They check your papers, your cargo manifest, stuff like that. If you're overweight, they ground you; and you can't deliver your cargo. Costs the company a bundle."

"Can I try the takeoff?"

"Sure. It's a short runway, but there's no wind. Just remember to push your throttles forward faster. Stand on the brakes a bit while you push the engine speed."

Matt followed his instructions. The plane rocked as the RPM's increased.

"Now!"

Matt pulled his feet off the brakes. The straining plane accelerated rapidly. The thrust pushed his head back into the seat. They sped toward the fence. Matt lightened the nose, then pulled the craft off the runway, and they were over the fence. As the Cessna climbed through the air, Matt turned the plane east for New York City.

"You're entering the busiest airspace in the nation," Tom said, pointing to city lights below them. "Teterboro's in Jersey, just across the Hudson River from New York."

As they neared New York City, amber lights illuminated the ground, stretching into the distance. Beyond the lights lay the empty darkness of the Atlantic Ocean.

"Long Island. Go left up the Hudson. There's the Statue of Liberty."

Matt could easily make out the historic landmark four thousand feet down. "As close as we are in P.A., I've never seen it before."

Tom nodded as he followed tower directions for landing. The ramp area for the freighter planes was crowded. Tom took the 310 down the rows of waiting planes and neatly fitted the Cessna between two other parked planes.

A man in his early thirties ran up. "Here comes the boss," Tom explained. "Don't let Van Ryck get to you. He thinks he's going to make Flying Dutchman the next major air freight service in the northeast—all by himself."

They were out of the craft by the time Van Ryck got there. "How's business?" Tom asked.

Van Ryck nodded at the line of 310's. "It's a mess! We got ramped earlier tonight. We were overweight, and I've had to split two loads. You've got a load for Harrisburg. It's got to be there as soon as you can beat it back."

"I'll need a couple hundred pounds of fuel before I take off."

"Haven't you got enough to get back without refueling?" Van Ryck demanded as ground crewmen quickly unloaded and reloaded the plane.

"Not according to FAA specs."

"I'm sick of FAA specs! This load delay is costing me plenty in penalties."

"What'll a crash cost you?"

"All right! Get your fuel."

Tom winked at Matt and led him inside to order their fuel from the Fixed Base Operator. "Someday, I'll have an FBO," Tom said. "I've been saving for a down payment. When I get too old to enjoy flying every night, I'll just run my FBO and give a few lessons."

"Sounds great," Matt responded.

"I'm not ready to be tied down yet, but the time will come." Tom stepped to the counter and showed his credit card.

"You're after the Navajo," the lady responded as Tom signed the chit. Van Ryck met them outside. "Well?"

"We're right behind the Navajo."

Van Ryck nodded, then dashed off to meet another plane.

"He sure makes it tough on himself, doesn't he," Matt observed.

The fuel truck drove up. The driver grounded his hose, then unscrewed the fuel cap. Tom smiled and said, "I knew a case in Seattle once where a guy forgot to ground his hose. He was refueling a 707. Static electricity an inch long jumped from the wing to the nozzle. He jumped off the fuel elevator, broke both legs. By the time they had him out of there, all that was left of the plane was the skeleton."

They climbed into the 310. "I didn't know ordinary flying was that dangerous."

"Sometimes it's a whole lot worse," Tom said bitterly. "Get us out of here."

Matt lifted the plane into the sky. He was glad to be going home.

There were crosswinds when they landed at Harrisburg. Tom took the plane in carefully. A cold wind numbed their faces as they walked to the truck. Sleet began falling.

"What kind of weather keeps us from flying?"

"The only thing that stops us is when they close the airports."

"I wouldn't think pilots would want to fly in really bad weather."

"There's pretty stiff competition for flying jobs. This kind of flying is low on pay, high on experience."

Tom seemed depressed. Matt was about to ask why a man of his experience was doing such low-status flying, but Tom turned the radio to a late-night talk show, cutting off conversation.

8

"Matt! Matt!"

Matt rolled over and pulled the pillow over his head.

John's determined voice penetrated the thick layer of fiberfill. "Matt! Mom said to come and get you." John began tugging on the pillow.

Matt flung the pillow on the floor. "Can't a guy even sleep around here?" he protested.

"Nope," John answered cheerfully.

"What do you want?"

"Breakfast is ready. Mom says she'll take us to the mall. I want to go Christmas shopping. Come on. I already put jelly on your pancakes."

Matt dragged himself out of bed. His mouth tasted bad, and his leg ached. He stared at himself in the mirror. He didn't look as tired as he felt. He splashed water on his face and brushed his teeth.

When he got downstairs, Matt's mother was washing the counter. "Hi!" she said. "Hurry and eat. I can drop you and John at the mall for a couple of hours while I go to York."

Matt sat down at the table. He hated jelly on pancakes. He looked at John's cheerful face. It wasn't his fault. "Thanks, kid."

"Did you have a good flight?" Nancy asked.

"Pretty good. I got to do the takeoffs myself."

"Awesome!" John said. "Did you get to land the plane too?"

"Not alone. It'll be a long time before I can do that. We went all the way to New York City last night. I met Tom's boss."

"Brother Stratford," Nancy corrected.

"Are you gonna have some more pancakes?" John asked. " 'Cause if you aren't, I want them."

"Go ahead," Matt said. "I have to watch my weight."

"What for?" asked John. "Brother Stratford is big, and he still flies. Oh, for football."

Matt stopped eating. He realized he'd gone two days without thinking about football. Actually, he hadn't given it much thought since he'd talked to Beef. "The season's over, John. No more football until next summer."

"Gee, summer's a long time away."

"It's felt funny not going to your games this fall," Nancy said.

"Yeah," Matt said. "But there're other things in life."

"Like flying?"

"Like flying," Matt agreed. "There's also math."

"Math?" His mother looked at him in surprise.

"Dr. Samuels asked me to go to districts in math."

"Tell me about it in the car."

As they drove to the mall, Matt told his mother about the competition and then about his conversation with Tom. "Say, Mom, did you know that Brother Stratford has a master's degree in math? He went to Princeton."

Nancy looked thoughtful. "Did he? I thought maybe he was an airplane mechanic before he learned to fly. Some freight pilots get started that way."

"Heck no, Mom. He used to pilot jets for an airline on the West Coast. He flew Convairs for a commuter airline down in Florida, too."

"What in the world is he doing flying freight?" she asked.

"I haven't had the nerve to ask him. When I start talking about it, it's like a curtain comes down."

"Well, don't pry, Matt. When he gets to know us better,

maybe he'll tell us. I think I'll ask him to supper again tomorrow night. After all, it's Fast Sunday."

"Fast Sunday!" Matt and John both groaned.

"I hate Fast Sunday," said John.

"I don't see why. You're not even baptized. You don't have to fast unless you want to," Matt replied. "Me, I've got troubles."

"Why?"

"I invited Beef Kowalski to church tomorrow. Great!"

"Oh, I don't know. I think it's a good chance for people to see what the church is all about."

"Sure!" said Matt. "Sixteen little kids will say 'I'm thankful for my mommy and my daddy and the food I eat and the clothes I wear,' and some lady will get up and bawl. Beef will be really impressed! What am I going to do?"

"You could pray."

"What for?"

"It might help," she replied quietly as they turned into the mall. The parking lot already was jammed with cars. "Mr. Rawlins should be here soon. I'll stay long enough to get the helper started, then I'll go to York. I'll pick you up on the way home. That should give you time to do your shopping, John."

Inside the mall, Matt helped his mother remove dust covers from the booth. "How much money have you got, John?"

"4.57. I've been saving my allowance all fall."

Matt had been saving his too. It suddenly occurred to him that he was actually using his mother's money to buy her a present. Matt thought about it. He hadn't had a part-time job since he gave up his paper route when he made the j.v. team. His mom had spent a lot on scout camps, youth conferences, and athletics. He'd spent his time playing football. I'm not going to do it this year, he told himself. I'm going to earn some money.

Nancy Hansen walked around the booth. "Matt, Mr. Rawlins isn't here. If he doesn't come soon, I don't know what I'll do.

73

Do you think you could try it, just for today? I could take John to York with me if I have to."

"No way!"

Just then a sad-eyed older man with a red complexion shuffled up. "Sorry I'm late, Missus Hansen. I've been feeling pretty bad. Reckon that's why I overslept."

Matt's mother looked at Mr. Rawlins closely. What she saw seemed to reassure her. "I'm just glad you could come, Mr. Rawlins. Our Saturday Santa has quit. You'd better put your suit on. I have everything else ready."

"Missus Hansen, I can't stay past one o'clock. I've got a doctor's appointment down at that Apple-a-Day place."

"Oh dear. Matt, you'll simply have to help!"

"Mom, I've got an idea!" Matt said. His mother started to interrupt. "No, listen. Cindi works Friday nights and Saturday afternoons. Beef would jump at a chance to be with her. Let me call him."

She thought for a minute. "You know, Matt, it might work. Go call him."

Matt hurried across the mall to the public phones, looked up Beef's number, and dialed. "Beef, Matt Hansen here."

"What's happening, man?"

"I'm about to do you the favor of your life."

"I'm not sure I want to hear this one."

"Sure you do. How'd you like to earn $4.75 an hour being with Cindi Thompson every Friday night and Saturday from now until Christmas?"

"What's the catch?"

"My mom runs the Santa concession in the mall. You know, where kids come to get their pictures taken with Santa?"

"Yeah?"

"Well, Cindi takes the pictures. The Santa quit, and Mom needs somebody to take his place on Friday nights and Saturdays. Interested?"

"You bet! How come you don't want to do it yourself?"

"I'm flying Friday nights. Besides, I couldn't dress up and play Santa for all those kids."

"Oh, I don't know. I've done worse. Remember last year when we did *Oklahoma* at school? I played Jud Fry. For weeks, whenever anybody saw me, they'd sing 'Poor Jud is daid, a candle lights his haid.' "

"I don't remember that at all."

"Man, where were you last spring?"

"Thinking about football, I guess. I never knew you were into acting."

"I've been in a couple of school plays. It's cool being somebody else for a little while. When do you want me?"

"Come on down to the mall about noon. You can watch the other guy before you have to suit up."

"Sounds good. See you then."

Matt went back to the Santa booth. Mr. Rawlins was in his place, but there was no helper. His mother was behind the camera. When she finished, Matt walked over.

"It's all fixed, Mom. Beef jumped at the chance to work with Cindi."

"Good! Now if the helper would just get here. Could you fill in until she comes?"

"Sure, Mom. I watched Cindi the other night. You'd better show me about the camera, though."

His mother showed him how it worked.

"I can handle it, Mom," Matt replied. "Take John with you."

"But, Mom," John protested, "me and Matt are going Christmas shopping."

"I'm sorry, John. I've got to run the camera."

John's face crumpled. He began crying. "John," Nancy begged, "please, not here. We'll get a soft pretzel down at York."

"Tell you what," Matt added, "when you and Mom get back, we'll go shopping. I'll stake you to a video game."

John looked up. "Two?" he bargained.

"One," insisted Matt, "if you're good for Mom."

His mother hadn't been gone ten minutes when Tom Stratford strolled through the mall. He caught Matt's eye and ambled over. "How's it going?" He took a seat in one of the chairs set out for parents.

"It's getting busy."

"Where's your mom?"

"Down at the York mall."

A family came up. Their six-year-old boy readily climbed onto Santa's knee. Matt saw the old man wince, but he didn't say anything. After a short whispered conference, Santa reached into his sack and pulled out the coloring book provided for each child. Then he added a candy cane from a brown paper bag at his side.

"Thanks, Santa." The boy climbed down.

By this time, Matt had the photo placed into its folder. He gave the package to the waiting father, who handed him payment, right down to the penny.

"You know," said Tom, "playing Santa's good for me. I haven't been around kids in quite a while. If I'm going to be a good home teacher to your little brother, I'd better get used to kids."

Matt glanced at Tom out of the corner of his eye before he greeted the next family. There were twin girls, two slightly older brothers, and a set of harassed-looking parents. The mother was obviously pregnant and still on the young side of thirty.

Matt arranged a group photo in the small size. The parents were pleased with it. The camera had caught all four smiling, although their heads were less than half an inch across.

Tom spoke up, "That's a great picture."

"Thanks." The mother smiled. "My mother's alone now. I know she'll like it. I wish we could do something better, but Dave's been off work."

"Wait a minute," Tom said. "Let me give your family a Christmas gift. Put the kids back on Santa's lap and let's take a bigger picture."

The parents protested, but Tom overruled them. He turned to Matt, speaking quietly. "Shoot the $16.95 package, but put a different kid in each pose."

"There you go," Tom said as Matt handed the finished photos to the father. "Hope you get back to work soon."

"I'm going back after the first of the year. Thanks a lot."

"Merry Christmas!" Tom answered with a smile as the family walked away.

Santa spoke up. "You keep buying photos, and I keep giving candy away. That's no way to make a living."

"No," Tom agreed, "but it's a good way to make a life. See you all," he added and walked away.

"That's a good man," Mr. Rawlins said, "but something's sure eating on him."

Matt looked at him in surprise. It was their first exchange. "You think so?"

"Yeah," Mr. Rawlins said. He tightened his mouth. The false whiskers twitched. "I can always tell. I been there."

Matt looked up to see Beef making his way through the crowd. "Here comes Beef," he said.

"I'll stay on till one," Mr. Rawlins said. "You can kinda show him the ropes that way, and I can use the money. I'm saving for Christmas presents for my grandkids."

Beef watched as several families sent their children to visit Santa. Some were frightened. Mr. Rawlins didn't seem comfortable with them. He was better with the children who mounted his lap with confidence.

Beef sat in the helper's chair as Matt busied himself with

77

the camera. "The guy's no actor, but I think he likes kids. He just doesn't know what to do with them. I'll bet he doesn't have any."

"He must have one," Matt replied. "He said he was buying presents for his grandkids."

"They must live a long way off. He's not used to them."

"How come you're so sure?"

"In acting they teach you to study body language. I wonder if he's sick. He moves like it."

"That's all Mom would need. He's her weeknight Santa."

At one o'clock, Matt put up the "Santa is feeding his reindeer" sign. Beef followed Mr. Rawlins to the dressing room where Mr. Rawlins showed him how to adjust the costume.

"You won't need no padding," he said. "You're built like a football player."

"Right now I'm Santa." Beef sat quietly for a few minutes, feeling out the role. When he felt comfortable, he walked down the mall to his booth "ho, ho hoing" and waving to the children. Several families followed him back.

Business was so brisk that Matt hardly noticed when Cindi arrived.

She looked at the waiting line of families. "I'll handle the money, Matt, if you want to keep taking pictures."

"Why not? Might as well stick around until Mom shows up."

"Who's the Santa?"

"Beef Kowalski."

If Cindi was surprised, she hid it. She waved at Santa, and he nodded before lifting another child to his knee.

Mrs. Hansen returned before two. She glanced at the report sheet. "It looks as if business is going really well."

"We've been busy. How was it in York?"

"Real busy, but I've got a good crew down there. Brother Draybaugh is managing things for me, and there's been less hassle there than up here. Maybe I'm not as good a manager as I thought."

"You're just great, Sister Hansen," Cindi said.

"Thanks, dear. How's our new Santa?"

"Good," Matt said. "Turns out he's quite an actor. I must have been inspired." He grinned.

"Don't laugh," she replied. "I don't know about you, but I was praying we'd figure out something. Why don't you take John shopping? I'll help Cindi until you're through."

"Come on, kid," Matt said.

John skipped and hopped his way down the mall. Matt grabbed his arm. "Knock it off! You'll run into somebody."

"But, Matt," John complained, "all I've done all day is sit."

"How about if we go play a video game first?"

"Wow! Can we?"

They turned into the crowded arcade and threaded their way through the knots of people to an empty machine in the back. Matt put his money in the slot and got John settled playing "Paper Boy." Shouts of laughter drew his attention to a group of guys at a machine to Matt's right. A thin, dark-haired teen clapped a tall man on the shoulder.

"All right, you win," Matt heard him say. "Here's your money."

Matt assumed they were betting on the game. He turned back to John, whose game was nearly over. As they turned to go, John pulled on his sleeve. "Hey, Matt," he whispered, "what'd that tall guy give the other one?"

Matt turned to look. The group shifted, hiding the tall young man from view. Chico Cruz stood at the next machine. He looked disgusted.

"Tough luck?" Matt asked.

Chico seemed surprised to see him. "I'm checking out what Dr. Samuels calls mathematical probabilities."

79

"My kid brother likes to play too," Matt said. "I'm taking care of him."

"You're not taking care of me," John said. "We're Christmas shopping."

Matt shrugged his shoulders and grinned. Chico smiled back at him. "I am also with my brother," he told Matt. "Alfredo!" he said over his shoulder.

The tall young man came over. "Alfredo, this is my friend, Matt. I told you about him. He also likes mathematics."

"I remember," Alfredo replied. "You study to be a pilot."

Matt grinned in embarrassment. "I'm just learning. One of my friends flies freight shipments from Harrisburg International. I go with him and help unload cargo."

"It is exciting, this flying of freight?" Alfredo asked.

"Naw! We just load the boxes and unload them. No big deal."

"What do you carry?"

"I don't know much about the freight. Mid-Penn Couriers delivers our shipments to the airport. We just load the boxes in the plane and fly. Whoever wants to ship something calls them, I guess."

"Chico says you go to Buffalo."

Matt nodded.

"Hey, 'Fredo," someone interrupted.

"It is interesting to talk with the friend of my brother," Alfredo said as he turned to go.

"See you at school," Chico said.

"I like Chico," John said.

"I do too. He's in my math class."

"I don't like his brother. He has lizard eyes. I wonder what he gave that other guy?"

"Oh, who knows?" said Matt. "What do you want to get Mom for Christmas?"

Matt ruled out china figurines, perfume, and costume jewelry.

"Could I get her a dress?"

"Not with $4.57."

"I want to get her something," John wailed.

"Tell you what. I'll get paid $16.00 for working today. If we went together, we could get her a nice blouse or a skirt, maybe. What if we ask Cindi to help us pick one out?"

"Can we get it now, Matt?"

"Not today. I have to wait until I get my pay. Maybe I could even work some next week. Then we'd really have a lot."

"Well, okay. If you ask Cindi when we get back to the booth."

"You talk to Mom, and I will," Matt promised.

"Oh, Mom," Matt said about an hour later as they rode home, "Brother Stratford came by to see you."

"Did he say what he wanted?"

"Nope. He didn't say much. He bought a $16.95 package for a family."

"He's a good man."

9

BEEF KNOCKED ON MATT'S DOOR PROMPTLY AT twenty to nine.

"Come on in," Matt said. "Let me grab my tie." Matt quickly knotted his red tie and slipped into his suit jacket. "See you at church, Mom," Matt said as they ran down the steps.

Cindi was in the foyer with a group of Young Women when Matt and Beef came in. The girls crossed the foyer, and Cindi introduced them to Beef. LaMar, one of the priests, came in with his family. Matt snagged him as he went by.

"This is Beef Kowalski," he said, "our star lineman at Cumberland Ridge."

"Hi," LaMar responded.

"LaMar plays backetball for West High," Matt told Beef.

The three young men moved toward the chapel. "We have opening exercises in here," Matt said, "then we separate for classes."

"What are your exercises like?" Beef asked.

"Oh, you know, a hymn, a prayer, then some song practice."

"Actually, I didn't know. I've never been to a Mormon service before."

LaMar laughed. "I hear you, man. My cousins aren't Mormons, and they say visiting us is like going to another country. All the words mean different things."

Ten minutes later, the four left opening exercises for the classroom. Cindi sat between Beef and Matt. One or two of the other girls looked envious. Sister Goodman stood before the class. She was a heavy-set woman with grey hair. Her soft voice was easily drowned out, and sometimes the teenagers did just that. Matt hoped fervently that they wouldn't today.

Sister Goodman began, "Today we're going to discuss integrity. Would someone like to tell me what integrity means to him?"

Several made comments like "honesty" and "truthful." Matt raised his hand. "Integrity is doing what's right even when you know it's going to cost you," he said.

It was the first time he'd spoken in class since his accident. One of the younger girls nudged her neighbor. "Like, he can talk!" Matt didn't hear her, but Cindi did. She shot the offender an angry glance.

The discussion progressed to examples of integrity. "I always think about Joseph Smith when I think about integrity," Sister Goodman said. "You remember that he said he had seen a vision, and he knew that God knew it, and he didn't dare deny it, even though it led to his death. He bore the same testimony that Stephen, the first Christian martyr did, that he had seen God and Jesus Christ."

"If you'd actually seen Jesus, it would be easy to follow him," Jennifer said. "It's harder for us to have faith."

Cindi spoke up. "Oh, I don't know. Even great spiritual experiences fade in time. Look how alone Joseph Smith felt when he was in Liberty Jail, and what about Jesus on the cross? They still had to feel alone so that they could choose to be faithful. And that's what we have to do too. I think it's hard for all of us."

"You're right," Sister Goodman agreed. "Having integrity is hard for all of us, but it makes the difference in our eternal happiness."

As the boys went to priesthood opening exercises, Beef was thoughtful. Matt, Lamar, Wayne, and Beef joined Brother Thompson in the bishop's office for the priests quorum meeting.

Brother Thompson was friendly to Beef, but Matt thought he looked him over closely. Beef didn't seem to notice. Cindi's father wasn't articulate, but his sincerity was obvious. His large hands, scarred from his auto-body work, gestured as he illustrated his lesson.

Matt found himself noticing little things about the people, the building, and the meetings. He tried to see them through the eyes of an outsider. He wondered what Beef was thinking. Beef appeared to be interested. Matt hoped he wasn't just being polite. That wouldn't be good enough for Cindi.

In the few minutes before testimony meeting, Matt tried to explain it to Beef, to prepare him for what might happen.

"Who decides who's going to speak?"

"People decide for themselves."

"How do you know you should? I mean, have you?"

"Only once," Matt admitted. "I can't tell you how you know, you just do."

"What do you talk about?"

"People talk about their spiritual experiences, or things they're grateful for."

"Weird!"

"Oh, I don't know. It's different, I guess. But you get used to it." Matt's reply was more casual than his feelings. Would Beef think they were crazy?

After the meeting, the young people congregated in the foyer, but Beef kept looking out the doors.

"What's happening?" Matt asked.

"My dad might show up. We had a fight this morning. He wanted me to go with him to the country club to celebrate getting all-state. I told him I'd promised you and Cindi I was coming to church. He went off on churches, and I told him all he wanted was a trophy to show off to his friends. It got pretty ugly, but he didn't say I couldn't come. So I took a shower and came."

"I'm glad you did," Matt replied quietly.

"So'm I. I never met people like you guys before. Like that guy whose wife lost her baby and everybody helped them. I never saw a grown man cry before. It's different. I mean, he wasn't ashamed to let people know how he felt. That's cool!"

A sports car pulled into the parking lot, darting into a recently emptied space on the front row. It jerked to a stop, and a tall, solidly built man with sunglasses got out. When Matt turned, Beef had disappeared around the corner.

Cindi walked quickly to the foyer door and opened it for Mr. Kowalski. She took his hand and began shaking it. "Mr. Kowalski, it's good to see you! Thanks for letting Bill come. Everybody was so proud to meet him.

"Dad! Come meet Bill's father. Hey, you guys, this is Bill Kowalski's dad."

Her father came over and shook hands with Mr. Kowalski. "I enjoyed having your son in my class. He's a great boy, a fine athlete."

The youth rose to the challenge. They didn't know what was happening, but they sensed Cindi's urgency. "Great to see Beef," they said, or "Nice to meet you."

Cindi's father gathered several of the football-loving brethren around Beef's father and started discussing the season with him. Mr. Kowalski began to relax and talk with the group. "I came to get my son," he finally said. "My wife's waiting for us at the country club."

"No problem, Mr. Kowalski," Matt said. "I'll find him for you."

Matt walked down the hall toward the restrooms, peering into each classroom as he went by. He found Beef in the font room, sprawled in a chair at the end of a half-circle of chairs.

"Matt, what am I going to do? I expected a row when I got home, but I don't think I can handle one here."

"You and your dad really don't get along, do you?"

"We fight all the time. He's got a hot temper." Beef paused. "Well, I do too. You ought to know."

"I don't think he'll yell at you here. Cindi's got him busy shaking hands with all the football fans. He's either in a better mood, or he's in shock."

"Cindi's something else, isn't she?"

"She's uncanny," Matt agreed. "Sometimes I think she can see right through people."

When they returned to the foyer, they saw Mr. Kowalski, relaxed and smiling. "He's a salesman," Beef said. "If you can't control your feelings, you can't sell. He's still mad underneath."

Mr. Kowalski's face tightened when he saw Beef, but before he could say anything, Bishop Adams walked out of his office.

"Larry!" he exclaimed. "How are you doing?" The bishop stuck out his hand, and Mr. Kowalski took it.

"I didn't know you went to church here, Bruce."

Matt smiled. The bishop always talked about member missionary work, and here he was with a friend who didn't even know what church he went to. Matt would have to tease him about falling down on the job.

"It was great having your boy with us today, Larry."

The two men fell into an amiable discussion. Cindi and Matt took Beef to see the cultural hall.

"That's a funny name for a basketball court."

Cindi laughed. "Actually, we use this hall for everything. We play basketball and volleyball in the winter and have dances or ward dinners here. We even have plays." She pointed. "There's a stage up there."

Matt added, "We have Scouts in one of the rooms off the stage, and there's a softball diamond outside."

"They don't give you any time to get into trouble, do they?"

"Well," Matt replied, "you can always find trouble, but we do have a lot of fun."

Cindi gave him a sharp glance, but she didn't say anything.

Matt realized how little he'd taken advantage of what had been offered him. He stood at the free-throw line thinking of all the times he could have played basketball. They had really needed him to make up a team, but football had been his life. Well, it was too late for basketball this year, even if his leg would hold up. But when softball season rolled around, Matt would be there.

I wonder where Tom is, he thought. It's not like him to miss meetings. He walked into the hall, leaving Cindi and Beef talking. Bishop Adams and Mr. Kowalski were down near the Primary room, deep in conversation. Cindi's folks waited in the foyer. Matt found Tom's number in the ward directory hanging by the phone and punched the numbers.

Tom answered on the fifth ring with not much more than a grunt.

"Matt here. You all right?"

There was a pause at the other end. Then Tom replied, "Sure. Sure. Just a bit under the weather. I'll be fine in the morning."

"Anything I can do?"

"Nope. Everything's fine. Just a bad headache."

"Well, I wondered when you weren't at church."

"No, I'll be fine. Thanks for calling." He hung up.

Matt stood in the hall, phone in hand. He looked at the receiver. Had Tom given him the brush-off? He hung up the receiver just as Cindi and Beef came out of the cultural hall. Bishop Adams and Mr. Kowalski came down the hall. Beef's father was calm, even genial.

"Come on, Bill. Your mother's waiting for us at the club. I don't know about you, but I'm starved."

"Sure, Dad. Thanks for letting me come."

Mr. Kowalski cleared his throat. "Well, you know I wasn't too happy about it. If I'd known Bruce was minister here, I wouldn't have minded so much. Let's go, Bill."

"Bye, Matt, Cindi," Beef said. "See you tomorrow."

Matt turned to the bishop. "Boy, am I glad you guys are friends. Beef was sure his dad would throw a fit. Looks like you know him pretty well."

"I sure do. I handle all the insurance for his dealership as well as for his family. I don't suppose an insurance man knows much less about a family than their doctor or bishop." He shook hands with Brother Thompson.

"Come on, Dad," Cindi teased. "We can't wait on you all day."

"I'm just checking things out, girl. You're not figuring on dating that football player, are you?"

Cindi blushed. "Dad, we're just friends. He came to church with Matt."

"You may be just friends, but he isn't. I can tell. We don't need any nonmembers complicating things."

"Dad!" Cindi implored.

Bishop Adams said, "I don't think you need to worry, Brother Thompson."

"You don't, eh? Well, I can tell you're not her dad."

"She's a smart girl. She'll know what to do when the time comes."

"You sure of that?"

"Absolutely! That's why we teach these kids to go by the Spirit. Then when they need it, it's there."

"I sure hope you're right," Brother Thompson said, as he gathered his family.

Bishop Adams turned to Matt. "Your mom's gone. I told her I'd run you home."

"Thanks, Bishop."

"No problem. It's not far out of the way. Gives us a chance to talk a little. How're things working out? Evidently you talked to Bill Kowalski."

"You were right about him feeling sorry. It turned out to

be an accident after all. That makes all the difference in the world."

"How's that, Matt?" The bishop locked the front door, and they walked out to his car.

"I gave up a lot to play football, but it was what I wanted to do. I did everything there was to do to be a top football player. I punched my ticket. I couldn't stand somebody else taking it away from me. But an accident's easier to take, somehow. I don't mean I like the idea, Bishop, but I can handle it."

The bishop stopped the car when the street teed into the highway. He waited for a string of cars to pass. "Matt, I ought to quit while I'm ahead, but this idea that you just punch your ticket and get the right results bothers me. You heard enough in testimony meeting today to know it doesn't always work that way. Look at Brother and Sister Waller who lost their baby. They did all the right things: missions, temple marriage, keeping the commandments, wanting a child. They've been married five years, Matt, and still no baby.

"Or what about Brother Carstairs? He's always lived the Word of Wisdom, never smoked in his life. He just lost his left lung to cancer. Or Brent and Linda Jones who we're going to home teach. They've got a little girl with spina bifida. Which ticket didn't they punch?"

Matt was silent for a long time. Finally he said, "But Bishop, I don't understand. If doing all the right things doesn't get you what you want, what are you supposed to do?"

"You're supposed to do the right things anyway, Matt."

"Then what's the point?"

"What would you think of somebody who only did the right thing because there was something in it for him?"

"I see what you mean. I'd think he was pretty selfish."

"You got it, Matt! That's exactly what ticket puching is. Planning toward goals and working hard are something else entirely, though."

89

"What's the difference?"

"Maybe it's a question of arrogance, Matt. When we're dead set on doing what we want to do, we rob the Lord of his opportunity to lead us. He knows what's hidden in us and what we can become. We get so set on doing what we want that we forget that he may have other plans for us, eternal plans. We see only the now."

"But Bishop, what's the matter with football?"

"Nothing. It's a great game, but I'm not sure it's much of a life. You think about some of the pro-ball players you read about. Is that what you want for your life?"

Matt's conversation with Tom came back to him. With all his flying experience and education, Tom certainly wasn't where you'd expect him to be in his career. He remembered Tom's remark to Mr. Rawlins that they were trying to make a life.

"You know, Matt, you weren't a great football player."

"What?"

"You weren't, Matt. You were a competent player who gave so much of yourself and worked so hard that you really stood out in high-school ball. You might have done the same in college, but it wouldn't have been enough for professional football.

"You've already given your best to the game. You think about it, and you'll know it's true. You don't have that killer instinct—the will to win no matter who you have to step on. That's why thinking that someone would injure you on purpose got to you so much. Matt, you couldn't do that to someone else, but that's the order of the day in pro ball."

They drove in silence for a few minutes. The car slowed, then turned into Matt's driveway. "But Bishop, how do I find out what to do now?"

"You have to find the place in life that's right for you. When you find it, you'll know. Maybe it's time you asked Heavenly Father what he thinks."

Matt remembered another conversation he'd had with Tom. "Bishop, do you think my mom's found her place?"

"It's hard to judge, Matt. Eternally, I'm sure she has. She may still be looking for the here and now. There again, we're back to ticket punching. Sometimes you land at a different airport than you expected, and you have to change planes. Why do you ask?"

"Something Tom said when we were flying the other night."

"Tom knows a lot about changing planes," the bishop said cryptically.

10

Matt's mother was clearing the remains of dinner from the table when Matt came in. "I saved you some," she said. "Sit down. What took so long?"

Matt told her about Mr. Kowalski's visit to the church. "I don't know what would've happened if he hadn't met the bishop. It turns out they're friends. Beef's dad has a rotten temper, and they fight a lot." Matt paused to drink half a glass of apple-raspberry juice. "I'm sure glad Dad and I didn't fight."

Nancy sat down. "You know, Matt," she said quietly, "if your dad had lived, you might have done just that. Did you ever think about that?"

"We never fought."

"Of course you didn't. You were only eleven when he died. You were still walking in his footsteps, and that's flattering. But I've wondered sometimes what would have happened when you began making your own tracks."

"What do you mean?"

"As long as you followed in your dad's shadow, there was nothing to disagree over. But you're not a clone of your dad, even though you tried to be. You've got some of me in you, and a lot more of my dad. My dad was a good soldier, but he was a master sergeant. He wasn't nearly as ambitious as your father. He'd rather be with his men than with the brass. His men respected him, but they loved him too. They knew he'd be right down there in the mud with them. And he was, all through Korea and in Vietnam."

92

"I thought everybody in the service wanted to make rank."

Matt's mother smoothed a corner of the tablecloth. "Some people aren't cut out for the politics that goes into making rank. Your grandfather's one of those. He didn't have a lot of patience with the glory hunters, and none at all for the flyboys, which is what he called pilots."

"But Mom, flying fighter planes takes a lot of guts."

"He never denied that. He just said it was detached. You do your killing from a distance. And he used to say that when a pilot bought his farm, he went down in a blaze of glory."

"Like Dad?"

"Yes, Matt, like your dad. Your grandfather fought in the villages. He saw men not much older than you die or be maimed for life. Your dad saw the war from above the treetops. They looked at things very differently.

"He wasn't happy when I decided to marry a pilot. He learned to like your dad better, but he didn't believe in Matt's ticket-punching philosophy. Anything that got in the way of punching that ticket was expendable."

"You mean us, don't you, Mom?" Matt was really shaken. He was seeing a side of his parents' lives that he'd never dreamed existed.

"Sometimes it felt like it. Your father didn't have to go TDY when he was killed, but he went looking for those assignments. I thought my dad would have a lot to say about it, but all he said was, 'Nan, it's a damned shame he couldn't have been content to fly a desk for a few years.' "

"Why haven't you told me this before?"

"You didn't need to know."

"But, Mom, I thought you loved him."

"I did. But you can't live with somebody and not get to know them pretty well, unless you're purposely stupid. I knew where your dad had chinks in his armor. There were lots of

93

neat things about him too. He was so alive, so full of energy. Ambitious people usually are. They're exciting to be with.

"He took care of us; he looked ahead. Some pilots don't. They're the eternal optimists. Nothing will ever go wrong. Your dad knew it might, and he made sure we'd be provided for. He never looked at another woman, not even in Vietnam, all those years. His buddies used to tease him unmercifully about it. They called him the 'Rev.' "

"With all the divorces, lots of kids don't have both parents around," Matt said. "My social sciences teacher said that many of those kids have a lot of hidden anger. They feel deserted by the parent who's gone. I thought about that a lot. I don't think I'm mad at Dad, but I still remember that, when he left, we waved and waved, but he never looked back. Sometimes I wonder if he really loved me."

"He did. He was proud of you too. He just wasn't very good at showing it. That's why I think you two might have fought. He was so determined for you to punch the same tickets he did. We might have had a real battle when it came time for your mission."

"But Dad went on a mission."

"Yes, he did. Living by rules came naturally to him. He was friendly, and people liked him. He had lots of baptisms, but he resented the time he spent on his mission. In those days, you couldn't take two years off to go on a mission if you went to the Academy. So he felt he'd sacrificed the Academy for his mission. His commission was ROTC, and he could see that Academy officers did better when it came to making rank. Maybe that was behind his constant drive for promotion."

"I can understand that."

"So can I," his mother continued, "but he was letting it make him bitter. And that's dangerous. Sometimes we get mad at God when things don't seem fair. We rant and rave awhile, but if we keep on praying we get it all out. God can handle how we really feel; he wants us to tell him. But somewhere along the road, we've got to look beyond the problem to find what we're supposed to do next.

"Your father was a good man, but he was chasing the wrong goal. He told himself he was winning promotions for his family, but I wouldn't have cared whether he was an Air Force officer or a crop duster. It mattered only to him. He was glory hunting, and it killed him."

"You sound mad about it, Mom."

"I was. I was real mad at first, but I got over it. I kept thinking that if only your dad hadn't gone, if only he'd been willing to think about civilian life, we'd still have him with us. You have to watch out for the 'if onlies,' Matt. They'll destroy you if you let them. I might still be stuck with them, but something happened, and I woke up." Nancy paused, her eyes bright with tears. She stared out the window at a view long gone and far away.

Matt fidgeted, waiting for her to go on. Finally he broke the silence. "What happened, Mom?"

"Your dad told me he was sorry."

"You mean you saw him?"

"Like seeing a ghost? Of course not. But after he'd been gone a long time, one night while I was praying about it, asking why it had happened to us, your dad's voice came into my mind. I didn't hear anything physical, but it was as real to me as if I'd really heard him talking. He said, 'I'm sorry, Nan. I've really left it all up to you this time, haven't I?'

"I knew he realized how tough it was for me to raise you boys without him. Most important I knew he was sorry. I quit being mad, and I quit asking the wrong question. 'Why?' is the wrong question."

"Oh, I don't know. I'd sure like to know why I had to hurt my leg."

"After your dad died, I spent a lot of time at the temple.

95

One day it came to me that a long time might pass before I knew why. The question I should be asking instead was 'what?' What did Heavenly Father want me to do next?"

"Well?"

"Well, what?"

"What did you find out?"

"I'm still finding out. You do what comes next. In our case, that was getting John born safely and taking care of you boys. Now I'm beginning to wonder what else there is for me to do."

"That's what Bishop Adams and I were talking about on the way home."

"About what I'm supposed to be doing with my life?"

"No, Mom, about what I'm supposed to be doing with mine."

"What did he say?"

"He said I wouldn't be good enough to play pro ball, even if I hadn't hurt my leg."

"Why'd he say that? I think you've done very well."

"He said I'd already given all I had to give. You know, Mom, he's right. I worked an awful lot harder than someone like Beef. And he said I didn't have a killer instinct, that I couldn't run over other players to win."

"That's what I mean, Matt. That's your grandfather coming out. Your father wouldn't have hesitated. He might not have broken the rules, but he'd have had no mercy at all."

"Like look what happened to me, Mom. Would you want me to do that to someone else? I mean, if it hadn't been an accident."

"No, I wouldn't."

"The bishop's right. They do it in pro ball."

"Well, where do you go from here?"

"I don't know yet, but I'll find out."

Matt was still thinking about it when he went to school the

next morning. He'd never considered anything but football. He couldn't decide whether the world was so full of choices that he couldn't narrow them down, or just not full enough of things he really wanted to do.

When the bell rang at the close of math, Dr. Samuels called, "Mr. Cruz and Mr. Hansen, please remain after class." As the other students left the room, Matt and Chico gathered their books. The math instructor continued, "Have you decided whether you'll go to the district math competition?"

"I'd be proud to be on the team, if you think I'm good enough."

"I, also," Chico echoed.

Dr. Samuels smiled his faint smile. "Good. I've arranged for you to be excused from activity period to meet with me twice each week. I'll see you tomorrow. I expect great things from you both."

Chico smiled broadly as Dr. Samuels looked down at a sheet of paper on his desk. Matt whispered, "He sure was positive we'd accept."

"Who wouldn't?"

"Any number of people. Beef, for instance."

"I can't understand how Beef, who is so smart about some things, can have so much trouble with math. He doesn't believe he can understand. I try to convince him that he can, but it is hard. He must understand math if he is to go to college, no?"

"Not if he majors in football," Dr. Samuels interrupted drily. "Football is sufficient excuse for mediocrity, even in college. I hoped by teaching high school to impart some modicum of mathematical learning to young men before they reached college unable to do even a simple quadratic equation. I can't say I've been successful at enlarging the understanding of many football players, with the possible exception of you, Mr. Hansen. And, of course, you're not really a football player."

There it was again. First the bishop, now Dr. Samuels. Yet,

97

neither the bishop nor the instructor meant the remark un-
kindly. All these years Matt had seen himself as a football player
and as little else. "Dr. Samuels, if I'm not a football player,
who am I?"

"I don't know, Mr. Hansen. You show promise of some
ability to think. I hate to say potential, a cliché used to excuse
mediocre performance. 'But he had such potential,' " he mim-
icked. "I get angry whenever someone says that. The slowest
of us is born with more potential brainpower than Leonardo
da Vinci used. The question isn't your potential; it's what you
do with it."

In the three years that Matt had taken math from Dr. Samuels, he had never known him to talk so much. The most
personal comment he'd ever heard from him was "You did
well," or "You can do better than that, Mr. Hansen."

Being on the math team would be interesting just to see
what Dr. Samuels might say. Leonardo da Vinci . . . Was it possible that everyone in the world could be that smart? Matt had
seen pictures of his "Last Supper," and once he'd seen models
of da Vinci's inventions at the Museum of Scientific Discovery.
The guy'd invented a sumbarine hundreds of years ago.

Matt started to ask him about it, but Chico was off on another
track. "You're saying, Dr. Samuels, that it's not enough to be
intelligent. Perhaps you must be a man of honor?"

"Of course, Mr. Cruz, although I realize that my position
isn't a popular one. In today's society, it's enough just to make
money. No one pays much attention to the method you use.
You could be a drug runner, for example, and be looked up
to by some people if you were successful enough."

Chico drew a sharp breath. He started to reply, his face
troubled. He looked at Matt and fell silent.

As students for Dr. Samuels's next class began filing into
the room, Matt asked, "Who else is on the team?"

"Laura Satterfield," Dr. Samuels replied. "She's a student

in Mr. Butler's Algebra II class. My own choice was Miss Wong, but I suppose I was being selfish to expect the team to consist only of my students."

"Do you know Laura?" Chico asked as they left the room.

"Nope. Do you?"

"I've seen her. She is very pretty. I hope she's very smart also."

"Yeah. We'll need all the help we can get. Wouldn't it be great if we won at districts? I'll bet Dr. Samuels would be happy."

"Dr. Samuels isn't a happy man. But he would be pleased, yes."

Cindi and Beef were waiting for Matt when they entered the lunchroom. "Hey, Chico, man," Beef called.

"Come and eat with us," Matt said.

Chico looked pleased. "If I would not interrupt."

Matt realized that Chico's manners were unusually formal. Where had he learned his English? It was really old-fashioned. When the group had taken their trays to a table, Matt asked him.

"From my father," Chico said. "He was a professor at the University of Santo Domingo when I was small."

"I didn't know that," Beef said. The others were obviously interested, so Chico continued his story.

"He was Honors Professor of Mathematics. His students were the finest. He also was a man of research. He wrote books. Some of them were in English."

"How'd you ever end up here?" Matt asked.

"It's the story of many families in Cuba today. I don't usually talk about it."

"We don't mean to be nosy," Cindi said quickly.

"I don't mind. You are my friends. My father was a great man, a man of learning and of peace. For many years he ignored the politics of Cuba. He believed his work was all. When his

99

friends begged him to speak out, he refused. He said one must sometimes compromise. That was not wise."

"Sounds smart to me," said Beef.

"It is never wise to compromise with evil," Chico replied. "Evil always demands more than just compromise. But my father couldn't see that. He was content to compromise, as long as he was allowed to teach. Many times my mother warned him that to compromise was dangerous to his soul." Chico paused. "Please, you must not speak of this."

"Of course not," Cindi replied. Beef and Matt nodded in agreement.

"It was my brothers, Alfredo and Miguel. Cuba is part of the distribution chain of cocaine from Bolivia, Peru, and Colombia to the United States. Many revolutionary groups in South America are involved. Their financing comes from the sale of drugs. They pay huge bribes and kill people who speak out against the traffic. But Cuba exports revolution as it used to export sugar, all over the world. The drugs support the revolution."

"You mean the money?" Matt asked.

"Oh, yes, the money," Chico answered. "And also the corruption. The corruption provides more reasons for the revolutionaries to exist, and a population with many addicts is no longer a strong people. So the drugs are very important to the communists all over Latin America. Cuba is no exception, although Castro makes public statements against drugs and even executes people said to be drug runners."

"I read about that in the paper," Beef agreed.

"I don't believe what I read in the paper," Chico's voice became emphatic, "not when it comes from Cuba. I know better because that is what happened to my family."

"What do you mean?" Cindi asked.

"My brothers were involved in the shipment of drugs. Both are smart men, strong leaders, very important. My mother's heart was broken. My father realized that his compromise with the communists had taught his sons to cooperate with them. For a devout man, this was a great blow. He finally spoke out against the communists. He was well known; he had great prestige, so he had to be silenced. It wasn't enough for him to disappear, as so many have, into the prisons of Cuba. His reputation had to be destroyed." Chico paused again, his face twisted.

"My father was arrested and was accused of drug-running. My brothers were arrested too. They were put in the prison at Mariel. But their arrest was a fake. My father's wasn't. He was tried and sentenced to death.

"My mother was not allowed to see him. She sent me to my brothers to beg them to help our father, but it was too late. He had been executed. When I went to the prison to see my brothers, I was detained. It was the time of the Mariel Boatlift. Castro sent many prisoners on that boatlift. My brothers came to the United States, and I with them. Only my mother and my sisters are left in Cuba, and my father's name is now dishonored."

Tears of anger filled Chico's eyes. Cindi put her hand on Chico's arm. "It's not your father's fault. Your brothers had their own free agency."

"What is free agency?" Chico asked. "My brothers dishonored our family. My father is dead, and in shame. My mother's heart is broken. I am the only son left of my father. What can I do?"

"Well," Matt said firmly. "We can win the district math competition. Your father will be proud of you."

"My father will not even know."

"Oh, he'll know," said Cindi.

"But he's dead."

"His spirit isn't," Matt said. "He still knows you."

"Do you believe that?"

"Yes," Matt said slowly. He realized that he really did. "Yes!"

On Tuesday, Chico and Matt met at Dr. Samuels's classroom door. Laura Satterfield was already sitting near Dr. Samuels's desk. Matt caught his breath. Chico was mistaken—Laura Satterfield wasn't just very pretty, she was beautiful! She was petite, but her figure was more developed than Cindi's. Her eyes were a deep blue, although her hair was black. Her complexion was very fair.

"Come in," Dr. Samuels said. "Miss Satterfield, these two young men are Matt Hansen and Chico Cruz. They are the two finest students in my advanced placement calculus class."

"While I, of course, am only in second-year algebra," Laura replied.

"Mr. Butler says you're extremely gifted in mathematics. I hope he's correct."

Even in sarcasm, Laura's voice was as beautiful as the rest of her, a sort of southwestern drawl. She looked at Matt with approval but ignored Chico. "Let's get to work," she said to Matt, motioning him to a chair on the other side of her, leaving Chico to either take a chair behind her or sit on the other side of Dr. Samuels's desk.

Dr. Samuels saw Chico's dilemma. He rose from his desk, turned two chairs to face Matt and Laura, and motioned Chico to one of them. He stood behind the other chair, using it as a podium.

They began working problems. Laura *was* good; she seemed to take particular pride on the few occasions when she found her solution before Chico did. She was more willing to work as a team with Matt.

The hour drew to a close. When the bell sounded, Laura hurried from the room. Matt and Chico gathered up their papers more slowly. Chico looked thoughtful. "Dr. Samuels," he began, "I have been thinking that I won't be on the team."

Matt was startled. He understood how much the honor of

being on the team meant to Chico. "Hey, don't let her get to you."

"I'll speak with Mr. Butler," Dr. Samuels said. "It's vital that my team work together. As far as I'm concerned, you and Mr. Hansen are necessary. Miss Satterfield isn't. I'm not interested in her problems. I'm a mathematician, not a psychiatrist. If she doesn't contribute to the team effort, I can easily replace her. Mr. Butler may not like it, but the seniority system has its uses."

"You would do that for me, sir?"

"Of course," Dr. Samuels said, "and for your father. I've read his work. He was a great mathematician. You have talent. Whether you have his genius is yet to be seen."

"I did not know that anyone in the United States would remember my father."

"His name is on your school records, but perhaps only a mathematician would recognize it. I assume he's dead."

Matt held his breath.

"Yes, sir," Chico answered. "In Cuba several years ago."

"He'll be greatly missed," Dr. Samuels replied, no hint of question in his demeanor. "In the meantime —"

"Don't bother, Dr. Samuels. I'll remain on the team. My father would want me to."

"Great," Matt said, relieved that Dr. Samuels hadn't questioned Chico any further. "Let's eat lunch."

11

WHEN MATT'S ALARM RANG THURSDAY MORNING, he was sure John had been playing with it. It was too quiet outside to be 7:30. Matt pulled back the curtain. The street was covered with snow. Matt saw deep tracks where a few early-morning commuters had passed. He flipped on his radio.

"An early winter storm dumped more than six inches of snow on the mid-state area during the night," the announcer said. "Four to six more inches are expected by evening. And now for the school delays." He began the alphabetical list of delays and school closings. "Cumberland Ridge, two-hour delay, no morning kindergarten."

"Whee-oo," John hollered from the other room. He came running across the hall and hopped into Matt's bed. "Did'ja hear that, Matt? No school!"

"I heard. Move over if you're staying. I'm going back to sleep." He flicked off the radio and wormed his way back under the covers. John lay still for only a few minutes before he began wiggling. "If you can't be still, go play somewhere else," Matt said.

"Okay," John replied cheerfully. "I'll call you when Mom has breakfast ready."

"Don't bother," Matt said sleepily.

John went outside to make a snowman while his mother fixed breakfast. He rolled a lopsided ball underneath the kitchen window, then rolled a smaller ball and tried to lift it onto the larger one. When he couldn't, he laid it beside the larger ball. "Hey, Mom! Come look at my snowdog."

"I can see him from here."

"You can't really see him. Come out and pet him."

She sighed and picked up Matt's jacket from the chair where it hung. Wind blew snow across the floor as she opened the door. She stepped off the porch and carefully made her way behind the house.

"Boy, Mom, this is awesome! Look at the cars sliding on the road."

"This is a mess," his mother corrected as she watched the slow line of cars slipping on the wet snow. The township snowplow growled its way slowly along at the end of the line, scraping snow from the road and piling it in windrows along the sidewalk. "We'd better go in and wake Matt," she said. "He's going to have to dig out the driveway.

"Don't even bother to shower, Matt," she said from the bedroom door. "You'll need a bath to warm you up when you come in."

"Is it still snowing?" Matt asked as he pulled his jeans off the chair. He shoved his legs into them and stood up. He took a sweatshirt from the drawer.

"Only flurries, but the weatherman says more snow by tonight."

"Come see my snowdog," John called when Matt walked outdoors.

"Just as soon as I get the shovel from the garage." Matt opened the garage door, then walked back out with the shovel. "Hey, that's pretty good."

John grinned with pleasure. "He's got a long tail like Honeysuckle."

"He sure does. It's longer than he is. Hey, look." He put the shovel down. "What if we give him some ears and a long nose like Honeysuckle?"

Matt pushed two little piles of snow into points and made a collie-shaped nose on the end of the smaller ball.

"Wow! Now he really looks like a dog," John said. "Can I help you shovel snow?"

"We've got only one snow shovel."

"I'll get the garden shovel."

"Sure. Any snow you can shovel is that much less for me to move."

John ran to get the shovel while Matt started pitching wet snow into the yard. The windrow was three feet high and solid. Matt worked steadily at the cut he had made in the piled snow. John came back with the garden shovel.

"Where do you want me to start?"

"Right there. You throw your snow on that side of the driveway, and I'll throw mine over here. That way we won't get in each other's way."

John shoveled diligently, although each swing of his shovel moved only a tiny bit of snow compared to the huge scoops Matt flung onto the yard.

"You're doing great," Matt said.

"Boy, this is hard. I'm tired."

"Rest a minute, and you'll get your second wind."

"What's a second wind, Matt?"

"I'll tell you later. I can't talk and shovel snow at the same time." Matt turned back to the windrow.

John wandered off, but it wasn't long before he returned and shoveled a little more. Finally they cleared the entire driveway. Matt's hands were stiff, and his leg reminded him that it still wasn't well.

"The scrapple's almost ready," his mother said as the two came in. "Leave your shoes on the porch."

"Can't," Matt said. "The wind's blowing."

"Well, at least knock the snow off them and put them on the mat, or we'll have water all over the floor."

"I'm going to take a quick shower, Mom."

John and his mother were nearly through breakfast when Matt came downstairs. He grabbed a plate and loaded it with scrapple. "Is there any maple syrup?"

"Yep," John said. "But you got to eat eggs if you want syrup on your scrapple."

Matt took the tiniest possible serving of scrambled eggs. He poured a thin ribbon of syrup over the hot scrapple slices and sat down at the table. "You going to the malls today?"

"I'd better. John will have to go with me. Mrs. Bare has enough with her kindergartener home too. I just hope everyone can get in. Mr. Rawlins lives somewhere out in the country."

"How's he doing, Mom?"

"I'm proud of him. I'm almost sure he's stayed sober the whole time he's been working for me."

"Beef thought he was sick from the way he moved when he lifted kids."

"I've noticed that he seemed a little stiff."

"Oh, gosh, Mom, look at the time!" Matt jumped up from the table and grabbed his coat. His shoes were wet from shoveling. "John, run up and get my high-tops. Hurry!" He put his coat on and piled his books on the table by the door.

John came running downstairs. "Thanks, John," Matt said as he shoved his feet into his high-tops.

The bus crawled slowly down the road. Matt and the two girls from across the street waited behind a pile of plowed snow. The bus creaked to a stop, and they mounted its steps.

Almost twenty minutes later, the bus pulled up to the school. As Matt slid into his homeroom seat, the intercom crackled. "Homeroom period will be shortened to ten minutes. Activity period is cancelled. Please proceed as though this were day five of your schedule."

Drat, Matt thought. Now Chico and I will miss working with Dr. Samuels. Oh, well, I'll bet Chico won't mind not seeing

107

Laura Satterfield. I hope she doesn't keep acting like she did Tuesday.

During math, Chico sat in the corner. He didn't volunteer a single word during the entire period. Matt looked at him curiously as they left the room together. Chico had a scraped place high on his left cheek and his lip was swollen.

"Man, what happened to you?" Beef asked as they sat down in the cafeteria. "You look like you ran into a door."

"It's nothing," Chico said, dabbing at his lip. "Sometimes my brother Alfredo is mean, when he, uh," Chico paused, "when he gets angry," he finished quickly.

"What was he —" Matt stopped as Beef kicked him under the table.

"Here comes Cindi," Beef said.

"What do you think of all this snow?" she asked, sliding her tray across the table.

"Not much," Matt replied. "I must have shoveled a ton of it this morning."

"Is your mom going to York today?" Cindi asked. "I heard the freeway over Reeser's Summit is blocked."

"I don't think she'll try to go to York. She said Brother Draybaugh was doing a good job running things down there."

"Will you be able to fly tomorrow night?" Chico asked.

"We'll fly unless they close the airport."

"Do you think your mom likes Tom?" Cindi asked.

"I can't tell. I don't even know whether he likes her, but he can sure talk her into things nobody else can, like letting me fly. We never used to fly after Dad died. I told Tom she wouldn't let me. He just quietly said she would, and she did. It's weird."

"Maybe he's got a good line," Beef said.

"He doesn't talk much at all," Matt replied. "He's kind of laid back, but I get the feeling he never makes a move he didn't plan on. I've never met anybody like Tom before."

108

"Your father is dead too?" Chico asked.

"Yeah, just before I turned eleven. He was killed in a plane crash."

"Oh, yes, I remember you told me that when you told me you were learning to fly. It's strange. I study mathematics like my father, and you fly like yours."

"I played football like my father too. What else did your father do?"

"He played chess, but I don't like chess. It's too slow."

"My dad plays golf," Beef said, "and I feel the same way."

Cindi sat quietly. Matt realized that they were almost ignoring her. "What does your dad do for fun?"

"He doesn't have much time," Cindi said. "He works late a lot. He made a bird feeder for the backyard, and while he's eating breakfast, he watches them."

"I wouldn't have expected that. I thought he was a sports fan."

"He doesn't like TV. He used to go to Baltimore to watch the Orioles, but last summer he didn't go at all. Money's a problem, you know."

Beef looked at her in surprise. Among his family's friends, no one ever admitted being short of money, even when they were.

"Money can be a very big problem," Chico agreed. "Are you going away to college?"

"If I get a scholarship," Cindi said. "I've been saving since I was fourteen, but it's not enough."

"I need a scholarship too. Let's hope we both get them."

Matt realized how lucky he was. His only concern about getting a scholarship had been so that he could play football.

The bell rang, and students stampeded from the cafeteria. During fifth period, the principal announced early dismissal as heavy snow began to fall.

As Matt walked out the side door to catch his bus, he heard

a call from the parking lot. "Matt! Matt! We're here." It was John, leaning out the car window.

"What's up, Mom?" Matt asked.

"Mr. Rawlins's landlord called this morning. Mr. Rawlins is sick. Brother Stratford said he'd stay as late as he could to cover, but I thought we'd better go over to Mr. Rawlins's house. I'm worried about him."

"But, Mom, what if he's on a drunk?"

"John can stay in the car until we see whether everything's all right." Matt's mother pulled the car into the line of traffic waiting at the stoplight in front of the school. Snow continued falling steadily.

They cut across town on the bypass and drove slowly south on Lisburn Road. The narrow road curved among the hills. The last subdivision was three miles behind them when Matt's mother saw a narrow lane on her right. "This must be it."

"I don't think so, Mom. It just leads down to that junkyard."

"That's right. Mr. Rawlins is the night watchman."

The car slid on the snow as they drove down the winding lane toward the gates. The dilapidated trailer sagged against three young white oak trees. No lights showed. A battered gray Subaru rested beside the trailer.

"Do you want me to knock on the door?" Matt asked.

"We'll both go. John, you stay in the car until we call."

"If we call," Matt muttered under his breath.

Matt's mother rapped sharply on the door. No answer. "I think he's there. It doesn't feel like an empty house." She rapped again, then tried the door. It swung open. "Mr. Rawlins," she called into the gloom.

"Back here," a faint voice called from the rear of the trailer. Matt and his mother climbed the metal steps into the tiny trailer.

Cold, musty air assailed Matt's nose. Several overflowing bags of garbage leaned against the cupboard in the tiny kitchen. A torn sofa and a blond end table were the only furniture visible from the door.

Mrs. Hansen flicked on the forty-watt bulb. "It's Nancy Hansen, Mr. Rawlins," she called. "May I come in?"

"If you can get in," Mr. Rawlins replied.

Mrs. Hansen and Matt squeezed down the narrow hall past a cramped bathroom. Mr. Rawlins lay in the sagging double bed. Layers of blankets were piled on the bed. The room was bitingly cold.

"Mr. Rawlins, don't you have any heat?"

"I've got a kerosene stove, does me just fine. I ran out of kerosene last night. Didn't feel up to going after more at the station up the road."

"I can take our car. It will just take a minute," Matt offered.

"I'd be obliged if you would," the old man answered. "The can's on the counter. Money's in the silverware drawer."

Matt found the can in the kitchen. It was only a two-gallon can. Matt pulled open the silverware drawer. Two sealed envelopes from "Santa-in-the-Mall" were crammed in on top of the silverware. Matt lifted them out. Under the loose silverware lay a scattered pile of bills. A few were ones, but most were fives, tens, or twenties. Matt saw a couple of fifties. He pulled out a five and two ones, tucked the envelopes under the knives, and shut the drawer.

"Are we going home?" John asked as Matt opened the car door.

"Mr. Rawlins is sick in bed. We're going to get some kerosene for his heater. It's awful cold in there."

The car slipped and slid through the snow. "I'll bet no one ever plows this lane."

Matt braked carefully at the top of the hill and turned into the service station. "Fill this up with kerosene, please." He handed the battered can to the attendant.

111

"Sure," the long-haired youth replied. "Ain't that old man Rawlins's can?"

"Yeah. We were just up there. He's sick."

"You mean drunk."

"I said sick, and that's what I meant."

"Hey, man, no offense. If you'd seen him drunk as often as I have, you'd think so too."

"Does he drink a lot?"

"Man! Used to all the time. I haven't seen him drunk the last month or so though. He'd come in here drunk out of his mind and talk about the war. He's a strange dude."

"He's been working for my mom."

"Doing what?"

"She has the Santa concession at the mall. You know, where kids get their pictures taken on Santa's lap."

"No way!"

"Yeah. He wants to earn money for Christmas presents for his grandkids. He promised my mom he'd be sober, and he has been."

"Wonders never cease!" The attendant put the cap on the can. "I never heard him talk about grandkids, just the war. This do you?" He handed the can to Matt.

"You have another can I could take? I'd like to get him some to have on hand. He seems real sick."

"Sure," the attendant replied, flicking his hair away from his face. "Just tell him to bring this one back when he's done with it." He filled another can.

Matt stowed both cans in the trunk among the assorted junk his mom always kept there. A bottle of Windex and a roll of paper towels were left over from a car wash the youth had had last summer. The next time his mom hassled him about his room, he'd have to tease her about the trunk. But before he did, he'd better put the Windex away.

By the time Matt carried the two cans into the trailer, his

112

mother was heating soup on the electric stove. "Matt, see whether you can start the heater. I'll warm this up for Mr. Rawlins. He hasn't eaten all day."

Matt put the change in the drawer, filled the stove reservoir, and fiddled with it awhile before he got it lighted. Warmth spread out and filled the little trailer. As it did, odors from the garbage bags began to rise.

Mrs. Hansen checked the soup. "John, run out to the trunk and bring in the box of garbage bags. Let's get this stuff out of the way." She filled the sink with soapy water and looked around for a towel to lay the dishes on. She opened the silverware drawer. "Oh, my word!" She shut the drawer.

"That's what I thought, Mom," Matt said.

Matt found a dish towel on top of the fridge. His mother wiped off the counter and spread the towel, then he began to rinse the dishes. John came back into the trailer with the box of garbage bags.

Matt pulled out a large, black bag. He carefully lifted the sacks of garbage and dropped two of them into the plastic bag. He sealed it shut with a twist tie and reached for another one. John helped hold it open as Matt lifted the third sack carefully into the bag. The sack split, and coffee grounds, banana peels, and empty cans rolled across the floor. "Drat!"

"Never mind," his mother said. "This floor is three years past a good wash, anyway. You get the broom from the trunk, and I'll wash the floor." She poured the soup into a chipped cereal bowl, found an almost empty box of crackers in the cupboard, and carried them back to Mr. Rawlins.

"Thanks, Missus Hansen." He pulled himself up in bed, wincing as his back touched the wall. "Matt found the money for the kerosene all right, did he?"

"Oh, yes, Mr. Rawlins, he found the money. So could anybody else who walked in. Don't you think you should have it in the bank?"

"Don't trust banks. My daddy lost every dime he had in a bank during the depression. He'd've been better off to have stuffed it in the mattress. Who's going to look in a silverware drawer?"

"I hope you're right, Mr. Rawlins. While you're eating this, we'll straighten the kitchen up a little. I'll be back over tomorrow with some things to put in your fridge. You can heat them up when you're hungry. Don't worry about work. Tom Stratford said to tell you he'd stay until 7:30 tonight. If Beef can't come, we'll put up the reindeer sign."

"I hate to cause you all this trouble."

"It's no trouble, Mr. Rawlins. When I needed help, someone was there. Now we're here to help you. Next time you'll be helping someone else."

"I don't think so, Missus Hansen. I haven't been much help to anybody."

"People change, Mr. Rawlins. You've been a good Santa."

"I had to try, Missus Hansen. You gave me a chance when nobody in his right mind would have."

"All any of us can do is try."

"It's too little, too late. If that doctor's right, I don't have much time left."

"Mr. Rawlins, nobody knows how much time he has. We have to make the most of every minute. I've known people to live a long time after the doctors had given them up."

The spoon paused midway back to the bowl. "You mean well, Missus Hansen, but I've been in a lot of tough places. This feels different. When those tests come back, maybe I'll know more. I'm just trying to hang on and get enough together for my granddaughters to have a nice Christmas present. I never sent them one before. They'll sure be surprised. So will my boy. I haven't seen him but once since he got married."

"Where does your son live?"

"He's a cop down in Baltimore. His mama took him back

114

there when she left me. I was stationed in California, them days."

"I'm sorry," she replied as she straightened the covers.

"Nothing for you to be sorry about. She got lonely with me overseas. First she went to visiting the bars, then she got to having men friends. When I come back, we tried for a while, but I was drinking hard by then. He's a good boy, no thanks to either of us."

"I'm sure he'll be glad you thought of the girls."

"I don't know about that," Mr. Rawlins added, shifting position, "but the girls deserve to know their granddaddy thought something of them, even if it took a while."

"It's never too late for love, Mr. Rawlins."

"I hope you're right." He thrust his spoon back in the soup.

Matt had finished cleaning up the garbage and was washing the floor when his mother came into the kitchen. "I figured you might be a while."

"Thanks, Matt. You go ahead and finish. I'll take a minute and wipe out the fridge and wash off the cabinets."

She opened the tiny refrigerator. A can of evaporated milk, a box of margarine, and three hot dogs were all that were inside. "I told Mr. Rawlins I'd bring a few things over tomorrow. It looks as if he could use them."

John was getting bored sitting on the worn couch. "Mom, how much longer are we going to be?"

"Just a few minutes more."

"I want to help too. Mr. Rawlins is my friend."

"I don't think there's anything you can do right now."

"There're a roll of towels and a bottle of Windex in the trunk," Matt said. "He could wash the windows."

"Just like you and Cindi at Sister Haskell's. Is this a service project, Mom?"

"No," his mother replied, "it's just us helping a friend."

"Isn't that what a service project is?" Matt asked as John went out to the car.

12

THE WINTER DUSK HAD FALLEN BY THE TIME MATT and John carried out the garbage bags. Only a few flurries drifted down, but their tire tracks had filled. Matt brushed snow from the windshield. The car slipped and slid its way up the lane to Lisburn Road.

"Let's eat at the mall," Matt said. "We'll never get home and back again in time."

"Can we have pizza, Mom?"

"No, John. We'll eat at the cafeteria."

"Can I have spaghetti?"

"Yes, but you have to have a salad too."

"Who's going to be Santa when Tom has to leave?" Matt asked.

"I've been so busy worrying about Mr. Rawlins that I haven't had time to think. Maybe Beef could come in. Why don't you call him when we get to the mall?"

"Is Mr. Rawlins real sick, Mom?" John asked.

"I think so. He didn't say what was wrong, but he's waiting for tests from the doctor."

In spite of the heavy snowfall, the mall parking lot was nearly half full. Matt swung over by the dumpsters and emptied the garbage bags, then put the huge bag of dirty clothes into the trunk. A car pulled out near the main entrance to the mall. "No sense going around the other side, Mom. This is closer than the employees' parking."

Several minutes later, as they stood in the cafeteria line, Nancy asked, "What would you like to eat?"

"The meatloaf looks fine. I'll call Beef as soon as I get my tray filled."

They found a table near the front. Matt helped John tuck a napkin into the neck of his shirt. "Do I have to?" he complained.

"If you're going to the booth, you have to be clean," Matt said.

"I don't see why. I don't care if I'm dirty."

"I do!" Nancy and Matt said in unison.

They both laughed. "I'll go call Beef."

The phone rang several times. Matt was about to hang up when Beef picked up the phone.

"Beef, Matt here."

"How ya doing?"

"Not bad. Hey, we've been over to Mr. Rawlins. He's sick. Mom wants to know if you can come in. Tom's got to leave at 7:30."

"Man, I'd like to help, but my folks won't let me. I've got a big math test tomorrow. Why don't you do it?"

"Me?"

"Why not? All you have to do is put on the suit, sit in the chair, and hand out coloring books."

Suddenly Matt was ashamed. Dressing up like Santa Claus wasn't really such a big deal. Nobody would know him through the beard. If they did, he could handle it. "What do you say to the kids?"

"Pretend the boys are your little brother and the girls are that little girl at church, the one in the wheelchair. Pretty soon, you'll relax, and it'll be okay. You'll see. Everybody gets stage fright the first time."

"My mom will never believe this."

"Sure she will. She's got confidence in you. So do I, man. Break a leg!"

"No thanks. I've got just one good one left."

"That's stage talk. It means 'good luck.' "

"I hope!" Matt hung up the phone.

"Well, can he come?" Nancy asked as Matt slid into his place and picked up his fork.

"Nope. He's got a math test tomorrow."

"Oh, glory. I'll have to try one of the other Santas. Not that anyone would want to come on a night like this." She shook her head in disgust. "Snow!"

"But, Mom," John protested, "we have to have snow for Christmas. I like snow."

"You don't have to drive in it," Matt said.

"Neither do you. Mom can drive."

"Boys! That's enough. We've got a problem, and fussing at each other won't solve it."

"About the Santa, Mom, do you really think I could do it?"

"Of course you could, Matt. Beef's doing a fine job."

"But I'm not Beef! What if I say something really dumb?"

"You'll be in costume. Who'd ever know?"

"I will."

"You know, when you start reaching out to others you have an opportunity to give them a little of the spirit of Christmas. Concentrate on doing that, and you'll forget about being nervous."

"I'll help you," John said. "I'll sit on your lap, and you can practice."

"It's a deal!" Matt stood up, tray in hand. "Come on, John, let's clear this junk off the table."

"I'll stay a few minutes to get you started," Nancy said as they walked down the mall. "Then, if everything's going well, I'll take Mr. Rawlins's clothes to the laundromat across the road. John, you can help me sort."

"I want to stay with Matt."

"You can stay with me for a little while. But Mom will need your help with all those clothes."

"All right. If I have to."

"You two are being such good helpers tonight. I don't know what I'd do without you," Nancy said, winking at her older son.

No children were waiting to see Santa when the Hansens reached the booth. A slender blond woman sat fiddling with her purse. She stood up abruptly when she saw Matt's mother. She wasn't as young as Matt had first thought. Although she was attractive, she had fine lines around her eyes and mouth, and obviously her hair was bleached.

"How are you doing, Laura?" Nancy asked.

"It's been slower than molasses all night. Do you mind if I take a break?"

"Of course not. We'll put up the reindeer sign. Matt's going to take Mr. Stratford's place. He can go change while you're on break."

Tom stood up, stretched, and joined them.

"Thanks." Laura smiled at Tom. "I'll just get a cup of coffee. Would you like one, Tom?"

Tom looked at Nancy, who didn't seem seem to be paying attention. "No, thanks, Laura. I've got to talk to Nan."

Matt looked at Tom. His mother always called him Brother Stratford, although Tom occasionally called her Nancy. Matt had never heard him call her Nan before. No one had ever called his mother Nan, except his father.

A small smile appeared on Nancy's face. "I'll see you in fifteen minutes, Laura."

Laura looked from Tom to Nancy, then picked up her purse. She withdrew a cigarette and lit it as she left.

"This is the longest evening I've spent in a while," Tom said. "Is she new?"

"I hired her yesterday. Her name's Laura Satterfield. I think her daughter goes to Cumberland Ridge, Matt. Her husband's with the Treasury Department."

"IRS?" Tom asked.

"No, he's a drug agent. He's in charge of the regional task force."

"I hope Hal will be back to work Monday," Tom said. "How's he doing?"

"I can't tell. The boys and I went out there. He was in bed, but I'd say he was more in pain than just sick. He's waiting to get some test back, but he didn't say what they were looking for."

Tom turned to Matt. "So you finally got roped into this. How'd your mom manage that?"

"I decided it was time to quit being stupid."

"Anybody that can lift a 310 off in a crosswind, first try, ought to be able to sit in that Santa seat. It's not nearly as far to fall, even if you land on your face."

"Thanks a lot!" Matt said as they walked toward the dressing room.

"Not at all. I'd do the same for a friend." Tom replied. "Seriously, Matt, you'll do fine. And you're taking a load off your mom's mind."

"She's going to wash some clothes for Mr. Rawlins. I think she's really worried about him. She's taking some food and stuff over tomorrow."

"He doesn't look good," Tom agreed. "I'd say cancer, if you asked me."

"Do you think he'll be able to work next week?"

"I sure hope so. I'd hate to work with Mrs. Satterfield again."

"I know what you mean. Her daughter's on the math team with Chico and me. She's sure stuck up."

"Maybe she'll get over it."

"I wouldn't bet on it. You don't like her mother either."

"Mrs. Satterfield is probably a perfectly nice woman. She's used to being considered beautiful, and she expects admiration from men. What's inside her may be fine, but all you see is her outside, and I'm not impressed." Tom shucked the Santa suit. "Let's see what kind of a Santa you'll make."

The suit fit fairly well. Matt stood looking at himself in the mirror. "Tom, what do you say to these kids?"

"Don't promise them anything specific. We don't want any miserable kids come Christmas Day. Our job is to make them feel special. We want them to know they really matter. I'll be honest with you. Now and then you'll hear things that'll break your heart. Just for a minute, though, you can make that kid's life happier because someone cares about him."

"I didn't know what I was getting into."

"Neither did I, but I'm glad I did."

"Will you fly tonight?"

"How's the weather?"

"Why do you care? You fly anyway." Matt grinned.

"Not if they shut down the airport. What's it doing out there?"

"It quit snowing, but we got four or five inches more this afternoon."

"That might close the airport if they haven't been able to keep the runway clear. I'll give them a call before I go in."

"If you don't fly tonight, you can have your Santa suit back."

"Not on your life! It took too much effort to get you into it. I'll just go over to the laundromat, put my feet up, and keep your mom company."

Laura Satterfield had returned by the time Matt and Tom reached the booth. Matt looked at her closely, comparing her to his mom. They seemed about the same age, although a few gray hairs had begun to show in his mother's brown hair. Laura's mother might have gray hair too. Maybe that's why she bleached it. Mrs. Satterfield was about the same size as her daughter.

Matt's mother, while not really tall, looked big in comparison. Everything about Mrs. Satterfield looked planned, while Matt's mother looked alive. It was true that his mom didn't have much make-up on after the visit to Mr. Rawlins. She had a dark smudge across the sleeve of her white blouse. When his mother saw Matt and Tom, a smile lit up her face. Matt decided there was no contest. He'd take his mother any day.

"Here's Matt," Tom said. "Shall we put him to work?"

"Aren't you staying here, Nancy?" Mrs. Satterfield asked.

"I'll be back as soon as I can. I'm taking some clothes over to the laundromat for Mr. Rawlins."

"That's the skinny old man I worked with last night?"

"Yes, he is. He's quite ill."

"I thought he looked like an alcoholic."

"He has been. But right now, he's sick." She turned to go.

"Tell you what, Nan," Tom said, "I'll give the airport a call. If they've shut down, I'll go with you. Hang on a minute."

Tom went to the pay phones. He was back within a few minutes. "No such luck. We're flying tonight."

"You mean you'd rather take Nancy to the laundromat than fly?" Mrs. Satterfield said archly.

Tom looked at her with a smile. "That's a heck of a thing for a pilot to admit, isn't it? Come on, Nan, let's grab John and get that stuff over there before I have to leave."

"You don't have to do that," Matt heard his mother say as they walked away.

"I know it. I'm just a darned good home teacher."

Matt crossed the set and stepped up to Santa's chair. He sat down and leaned back. It wasn't the most comfortable chair he'd ever tried.

"What's a home teacher?" Laura's mother asked.

Matt tried to explain.

"Do you mean he's an assistant pastor?"

"Not exactly. We divide up the families in our church and

visit them each month. Just to see whether they need help or anything. Tom visits us."

"Oh, I thought maybe he had a relationship with your mother."

"Sure. We're all real good friends."

"No, I mean a relationship."

He suddenly realized what she meant. "No way! They're just friends."

"Well, he doesn't seem very interested in women," she admitted.

"He keeps to himself," Matt said, "but he used to be married."

"I wonder what happened."

"I don't know," Matt said in his best cutting-off-conversation voice. He was glad to see a family approaching the booth. Matt took a deep breath. A little, red-haired boy about four sat on his lap. The list of toys he mentioned would have filled a page in Matt's log book. Matt wondered where he'd heard all the brand names.

"That's quite a list," he said in his best Santa voice. "What would you like most? If I give too many toys to one person, someone else might not get any." The boy narrowed his list slightly. "Merry Christmas," Matt said at last. "Don't forget to help your mom and dad." The visitor took the coloring book disdainfully and climbed down from Matt's knee.

Only a few children came to the booth. Most of them didn't want pictures. "Has it been like this all day?"

Mrs. Satterfield came back to his chair. "Just about. I've nearly lost my mind. Time goes so slowly."

Matt agreed. "The only time I worked the camera was a Saturday, and we were about run off our feet."

"It's better to be busy. It keeps you from thinking."

At one time, Matt wouldn't have understood what she meant, but after the past few months, he knew how she felt.

He searched for something to say. "I've met your daughter," he said finally.

"You have?"

"Last Tuesday. She's on my math team. She's real smart."

"She's a very pretty girl too," Mrs. Satterfield added.

Matt thought about Tom's assessment of Mrs. Satterfield. He looked at her closely. "Yes, she is. She looks like you."

"Why, thank you. We used to look a lot more alike before I got old and gray." She laughed a brittle little laugh. "That's when I became a blond. It's hard to stay pretty at my age."

Matt found himself feeling sorry for her. His mother didn't seem to worry very much about her looks. "Well, if Laura takes after you, she'll be all right," he said. He wished Cindi were here. She'd have known just what to say.

"You must be the boy Laura told me about. She was really impressed with you. Who's the Mexican boy? Laura was surprised he was on the team."

Matt thought quickly. Was Mrs. Satterfield as much of a snob as her daughter? Maybe he could do Chico a favor and get Laura off his back.

"You must mean Chico Cruz. He's Cuban." How far did he dare go? "His father was a university professor, a famous mathematician. Dr. Samuels says he was a genius."

"Dr. Samuels knows his father?"

Matt's truthful soul took hold. "Knew of him, yes. He's dead now."

Mrs. Satterfield digested the information. "Perhaps he's on the team as a tribute to his father."

"Oh, no! Dr. Samuels thinks Chico is real smart. He said so."

Several more children came, and Mrs. Satterfield took a few pictures. Matt found he really could relax and talk to the kids.

Nancy came back with John. She sat talking with Mrs. Satterfield for a few minutes. "How long have you been here?" Nancy asked.

"Since June."

"Do you like Pennsylvania?"

"Not very well, but you know how it is. When promotions are offered, you take them. I'm a Texas gal myself. I'd just as soon stayed in Austin, but Don would never be satisfied to be deputy there when he could be chief here."

"Ticket punching," Nancy agreed. "My husband was military. I know what you mean." She looked at the dwindling crowd. "Let's close up and go home."

"Sounds good," Matt agreed.

"I'd rather the miss the money than be bored to death," Mrs. Satterfield said. By the time Matt returned from the dressing room, the two women, with John's help, had covered the booth for the night.

"I'm hungry," John said as they walked past the pizza shop.

"I'll treat everybody to a slice of pizza," Nancy offered.

"Thanks, but I'm watching my weight," Mrs. Satterfield said. "You know how it is. If I don't watch my figure, nobody else will."

Matt and John ordered pepperoni and mushroom. Nancy ordered a diet soda. "Matt, how'd you get along with Laura?"

"All right, I guess. She sure worries a lot about her looks. Tom doesn't like to work with her either. He said she didn't impress him."

"Maybe I'll have a slice of pizza after all."

13

THE MAIN ROADS WERE CLEARED WHEN MATT AND TOM left for the airport Friday night, but ice and snow covered the secondary roads.

"You think we'll get more snow?" Matt asked.

"They're not expecting any more this far west. Buffalo's cloudy, but the airport's open. There's a storm in Jersey, but that won't bother us."

Twenty minutes later, they pulled into the airport parking lot. A stiff wind blew from down river, and Matt huddled deeper into his winter coat. Tom held the flashlight while Matt did the checks.

Matt climbed the wing, opened the door, and passed over the right seat. He reached between his legs and pulled the lever to adjust his seat as Tom settled himself. Matt flipped on the four batteries one after another. The magnetoes sprang into life.

"Let the fuel pump prime for fifteen seconds, since it's so cold."

The left engine coughed, then fired. Matt eased the throttle back. The right engine refused to catch.

"Pump it a couple of times."

Matt gave the throttle a couple of quick strokes forward and back; the engine finally caught. He eased the 310 between the rows of planes, circled to the left, and maneuvered near the building. He turned the plane 180 degrees and killed the engines. They waited for the courier.

"It's too cold out there," Matt said. "Let's stay in here until we see him coming." They waited in the darkness, only their marker lights flashing. Matt saw the van first. They clambered out and opened the cargo door while the van backed into position.

"Cold night for flying," commented the driver as he opened his doors.

"Well, we've got heaters," Tom said cheerfully.

"Things are a mess in South Jersey," the courier said. "They got an ice storm late this afternoon."

"That's what I heard, but it won't bother us. The weather's okay in Buffalo, and we're only going to Pottstown."

"How come you're not flying checks tonight?"

"I had radio problems last night. The guys were working on them most of the day. Hank took the checks last night. He must have taken them again."

"Yeah, he did. You'll have a short night tonight."

"Sounds like it. Glad there's a load for Buffalo." Tom peered into the van. "That looks like a lot of weight."

"It's not over capacity. The boss isn't about to get you ramped."

"Okay, put this Cruise, International stuff in the nose."

"Here you are. Cruise, International."

"What?" Matt said.

"Cruise, International. Must be some kind of travel company."

"Oh." Matt lifted a square box into the nose.

The courier slammed the doors of the empty van. Tom radioed ground control for taxi clearance. Matt maneuvered the plane along the ramp to the engine run-up area.

Landing lights blazed as a 707 passed over the cooling towers of Three Mile Island. The plane dropped past them out of the sky. The radio came to life, "Flying Dutchman 2407, you're cleared for takeoff."

"Roger," Tom replied. "Let's go, Matt."

Matt switched on the landing lights. The beams rotated in their sockets, and the area in front of the plane sprang into bold relief. He rocked his feet back, freeing the brakes, then pushed the right pedal. The 310 swung onto the runway, almost exactly over the lights buried down the middle. A thrill went through him as he felt the wheels leave the runway. The 310 climbed steadily into the night sky, and the lights below dropped away. He cut the landing lights. Matt brought the wheels up as Tom made the final turn. The plane continued climbing until it reached eight thousand feet.

They flew northwest toward Buffalo, above a thick layer of clouds. Tom spoke, "At this altitude, we've got a forty-mile-an-hour wind from the west. If we used only the compass, we'd be blown way off course. We have to compensate for the wind. Without the radio signals to follow, we couldn't fly at night, or even in the daytime if it were cloudy."

The plane pitched and rocked as they neared Buffalo. They dropped to five thousand feet, then to four thousand, then into the clouds below. It was like flying in a dream, Matt thought. But what if they ran out of sky before they ran out of clouds?

At two thousand feet, they broke through the cloud cover. Buffalo lay below, carpeting the darkness with its pinpoints of light.

"Okay, Matt, do as much of the landing as you can."

Matt pulled the throttles back, and the plane slowed to 140 knots.

"Good. We're on the downwind leg of our approach."

Matt reached below the throttles and pulled the flaps lever into the first notch. The plane shuddered and slowed.

"We're abeam of the airport, and we're at 140. Drop the landing gear."

Matt felt the reassuring thump as the three wheels dropped

into place. Turbulence increased as their speed dropped to 120.

They made a ninety-degree turn to the right. "Put on full flaps," Tom continued, "and make your final approach at about ninety."

The Cessna slowed further, and they turned for their final approach. The runway rushed up to meet them. As slow as they were going, Matt realized he'd never driven a car this fast.

"All right, Matt. I'll take it from here, but stay on the controls."

Matt felt Tom's delicate touch through the controls as they crossed over the runway threshold markings and touched down. Tom turned the controls back to Matt, who followed Taxiway Bravo to the far end of the massive building. He turned near the fence, following it briefly, before turning the plane nose out. Matt killed the engines, switched off the lights, set the brakes, and inserted the gustlock.

"You've got a pilot's touch, Matt. All it's going to take is experience."

"There's a lot to remember," he replied, pulling up his hood and stepping down the wing onto the concrete. Morrison's Aztec was parked nearby. They walked across the concrete to the building and found hampers for their load.

Tom opened the side door and began loading boxes into the hamper. Matt reached up to open the forward compartment. The load consisted of a half-dozen heavy, smallish boxes. He placed them in the second hamper and slammed the door shut. They pushed the cargo across the concrete, through the doors, and across the building where the courier would pick them up.

Morrison walked in. "Didn't figure you'd fly through the storm," the lanky Canadian said.

"All the heavy weather's east of Harrisburg," Tom replied.

"Lucky you! My airport's closed. I'll probably be here all night, waiting for the fog to clear. "How's the flying, kid?"

"Super!"

"You've got one of the best instructors in the business. I still think you should get an FBO, Stratford. You're a born teacher. It's good to see you at it."

"Maybe so, but I'd rather fly. They'll have to make me quit."

"How's the headache?"

"It's gone. I was under the weather for a couple of days, though. It hurt so bad I was seeing double Sunday morning."

"What did the doctor say?" Matt asked.

"I didn't go. I just had my physical two months ago. Must have been a flu bug. By Monday I was ready to fly."

Morrison leaned against the door. "Well, I'm glad to see you still in the air. I'd sure like to see you instructing, though. You'll never get rich like this."

"I'd never get rich teaching, either."

The courier drove up with the shipment for Pottstown. Morrison helped them unload the boxes and transfer the ones from Tom's hamper to the van. Matt brought his hamper over.

The courier rejected them. "They're not mine. Leave them here. Somebody will be along to pick them up."

They left the boxes on a pallet while they loaded the medical tests into the two hampers. "Thanks for your help, Morrison," Tom said. They trundled the hampers down the hall and to the waiting Cessna.

"No need to load the nose. This stuff's light," Tom said as they stacked the boxes in the cargo area behind their seats. They pushed the empty hampers back inside the building. "We might just as well take them across. Save somebody doing it later."

Morrison wasn't around. The boxes they'd left stacked on the pallet were gone.

"Somebody must have picked them up already," Matt said.

130

"Must have," Tom agreed.

"What if somebody stole them?"

"Not likely. You'd have to know what was worth stealing. Like those canceled checks — they've got a book value of $80 million, but what would you give for them?"

"I see what you mean."

Matt walked through the door into the hall, looking for the drinking fountain. He passed the office. Morrison had his back to the door as he talked on the phone. "It just got here. I'll bring it up as soon as I get clearance. The airport's fogged in. I can't land." He paused. "Of course I'll be careful. Do you think I'm nuts?"

Matt walked on down the hall to the water fountain.

"I told you, I'm careful. I've been inside before," Morrison said as Matt bent his head over the drinking fountain. The fountain whirred. He took several sips, wiped his mouth with his hand, and turned back up the hall. Morrison stood in the office doorway, a scowl on his face.

"Oh, it's you, kid." He seemed relieved. "I didn't know anyone was around until I heard the fountain."

"Just getting a drink," Matt replied and kept on walking.

Morrison took a step toward Matt. He stopped when the door at the end of the hall opened. It was Tom.

"Ready, Matt? Good luck getting out, Morrison."

"Getting out's no problem; it's getting in that's keeping me on the ground. No sense going aloft and flying around all night."

"That's for sure. Let's go, Matt. See you next week."

At the end of the apron, Tom contacted ground control and received clearance. Matt swung onto the runway, positioning the 310 directly over the lights.

"It's all yours, Matt."

Matt's feet were light on the pedals. He eased the throttles forward, maintaining a steady acceleration as the Cessna twin

131

gathered speed. The runway lights flashed rapidly underneath him.

Aloft, turbulent air kept Matt too busy to ask the questions nagging at him about the extra cargo they'd taken to Buffalo. As they neared Pottstown and dropped altitude, they ran into a driving snowstorm. Thick flakes slashed toward the windshield, to be whipped over the cockpit by the air stream. Tom continued his patient instruction. Morrison was right, Tom was a born teacher. Matt wondered why Tom didn't want to teach. He seemed to enjoy it.

"This is thick," Tom admitted. "See the green beacon anywhere?"

Matt looked around, but he couldn't see it. Normally, the cooling towers of the Limerick nuclear plant were a good guide, but tonight they were hidden by the snow. They flew several minutes, then banked again. Fuel gauges dropped as they searched for the dark airport. Matt grew more nervous, but Tom seemed calm. Matt spoke first, "I sure wish the runway lights were on. We might be able to see them."

"It might help," Tom agreed.

Matt caught a flash of green from the corner of his eye. "There it is!" he pointed.

"Sure enough," Tom said. "I'll take her in."

He turned the craft toward the beckoning light. Snow slammed toward them. Tom keyed the mike, and runway lights flashed on. He took the plane in, cutting through snowdrifts on the short runway. Crosswinds buffeted them, whipping the snow into drifts, lifting it and rearranging it, but Tom held the craft steady. He turned the plane and taxied up to the building. They climbed out into the darkness.

"Boy, this place looks deserted," Matt said as they walked through the snow to the building. As he reached for the door, it swung open. Keys in hand, Vic came out.

"What are you doing here, Tom? I left word in Buffalo that

we were closed. You're supposed to take that load to Philly International."

Tom muttered under his breath. "Nobody in Buffalo said anything about a message. What time did you call?"

"Oh, about eleven, I guess."

"You know I'm due there at 10:30. If I'm on schedule, I'm out of there at 10:50. Don't you think calling at eleven's cutting it just a bit close?"

"Calm down, Tom. No problem. It's just a short hop over to Philly."

"You don't call landing a plane in a crosswind, on a short runway covered with snow, at an airport that's closed, a problem? Just what would you call a problem — flipping the plane into a snowbank?"

"Look, Tom, I'm sorry. We've been shifting plans and schedules all night. South Jersey's iced in; we can't get a plane out of there. Everything's a mess. I've had Van Ryck on the phone screaming at me half the night."

"Anybody bother to notify Philly that Pottstown's closed? They've got my flight plan. I was on the air with them until I dropped down, and they didn't say a word."

"It's a city-owned airport, Tom. Somebody should have called them."

"Doesn't look like anyone bothered. Maybe you'd better call them."

Vic unlocked the door. "Yeah, I'd better. Sorry for the foul-up." He went back into the building. Tom and Matt climbed into the Cessna.

"Oh, well, here we go again," Tom said as he took the plane to the far end of the runway. He spun the craft around in the snow. "This is a heck of a way to run a flight service. If Van Ryck doesn't get it together, he'll either lose his contracts, or the FAA'll shut him down."

He stood on the brakes and revved the engines. "Hang on, Matt."

The 310 strained and quaked against the brakes. Tom released them, and the plane shot forward. Each drift they hit slowed the 310 slightly. The twin engines strained to gain speed through the deeper snow near the end of the runway.

The fence sprang at them. Matt didn't dare look. He imagined the Cessna breaking through the chainlink fence, roaring out onto the highway. He wondered what he should do to prepare for a crash. His eyes snapped shut.

Matt felt the plane pull sharply up into the sky. As he opened his eyes, the fence dropped below them. There was a half-smile on Tom's face. "Scared, Matt? Don't worry. It doesn't get much worse than this, ever."

Tom keyed Philadephia for landing clearance. A female voice came on. "You have a twenty-minute wait," she said, giving circling instructions.

"We don't have twenty minutes reserve fuel," Tom answered.

"Why not?"

"We were going to refuel in Pottstown; it's closed."

The voiced sighed. "Okay, come on in. We'll divert the other traffic."

Tom showed Matt how to change fuel lines in mid-air as he husbanded the fuel in his reserve tanks.

"Fuel's heavy. Van Ryck doesn't like wasting money hauling fuel from airport to airport. We run lower than I like. Between the time we spent looking for the Pottstown airport, and the flight over here, we're right on empty. Good thing I keep a bigger reserve than Van Ryck thinks I should."

After the short, snow-clogged runway at Pottstown with its crosswind, Matt felt relieved to be landing on the long, well-lit, snow-free runway. "This sure beats Pottstown."

"You bet," Tom replied. "There's nothing I hate worse than crosswind landings."

14

As THEY TAXIED TOWARD THE FREIGHT TERMINAL, they passed a Mitsubishi ME-2 being towed away. Its wings sagged, nearly touching the ground. Tom pointed. "See that? The pilot landed too hard and flexed his wings. Looks as though he broke the main spar."

"Do you think he's hurt?"

"Maybe not physically, but he's in a world of trouble. There'll be an FAA inquiry. Insurance agents will flock around, and he'll probably lose his job."

"Will he have to quit flying?"

"Depends on his record. I knew a case down in Texas once where a guy hired a pilot after a crash. Said he didn't want any hotshot pilots playing demolition derby with his planes. He figured a guy who'd had a crash was apt to be more careful."

"Did it work?"

"I guess so. The pilot hasn't crashed since then. I tell you, Matt, one airplane crash is all you ever want."

Was Tom himself the case down in Texas? Matt remembered that he'd worked there. Matt was trying to get up nerve to ask him, but they completed their taxi to the waiting van.

"What took you guys so long?"

"Nobody bothered to tell us Pottstown was closed."

"Man, everything's closed. I won't get five miles on the roads around here. This load won't make it to the lab before morning."

Tom and Matt helped load the boxes. "I nearly forgot. Call

135

your office in Teterboro." The driver slammed the door shut and started the engine.

Tom dug out his credit calling card. "I'll be right back."

Matt wandered over to the FBO. In a few minutes Tom came in. "So much for a short night," he said. "Fill the main tanks and the auxes," he told the duty person.

"Sure thing. There's a couple of planes ahead of you, though." The operator picked up the microphone, relaying instructions to the fuel truck.

Tom and Matt found a soda machine. Tom pulled out two cans of root beer and tossed one to Matt.

"What's happening?"

"We're going to Teterboro to pick up a load for Logan Airport in Boston. The Navaho they usually send got caught in the ice storm in Vineland. It's going to be a long night. I called your mom and told her we'd be late."

"What'd she say?"

"Not much, why?"

Matt hardly knew what he wanted to say. "Oh, I don't know. You can get her to agree to stuff she'd sure scream about if I tried."

"She seems easy enough to get along with to me."

"Maybe that's what I mean. She's usually more uptight."

"Who knows?" Tom shrugged.

"Don't you ever wonder about things, Tom?"

"Everybody does. Some things, there's no use wondering about—they just are. You just quit beating your head against the wall and accept them."

Matt sensed that they weren't talking about his mother anymore. He leaned back in his chair. He felt dead tired, and they had hours of flying ahead of them. He didn't care whether he ever flew into Pottstown again. Tom was a heck of a pilot to get them in and out on a night like this. He couldn't believe how different the weather was between Buffalo and Pottstown.

Buffalo! He sat up. "Tom, if a pilot thinks he's hauling something illegal, what should he do?"

"Report it. But he'd better have a good reason for thinking so. Why?"

"I think we hauled drugs to Buffalo tonight. And I think your Canadian friend is involved."

Tom stared at his empty root beer can. Matt told him about Chico Cruz and his brothers, outlining the death of Chico's father and the older brothers' involvement in international cocaine smuggling. "I know Chico's upset with them. Alfredo, that's the one I met, beat him up the other day. At the mall, John saw Alfredo hand a small package to someone. I didn't see that, but I saw him take money. And when Chico introduced us, Alfredo asked me all about the courier service. I think he was pumping me. I even told him the name of the courier service and that we went to Buffalo. He said he had a friend there. What if Morrison's his friend?"

"That's real tenuous, Matt."

"Morrison was on the phone when I went to get a drink. He said, 'It just got here.' Somebody kept telling him to be careful, and he kept saying he was. He said he'd been inside. Doesn't that mean in prison? And, Tom, the stuff we left on the pallet was gone. I don't think anybody else came in between the time we left it and when I got a drink."

"It could be a coincidence."

"I felt scared when Morrison started at me. I was glad when you came. I don't know why, it was just a feeling. Do you think I'm nuts?"

"No, I've learned to pay attention to my gut-level feelings. More'n likely they have nothing to do with our guts and everything to do with the Spirit."

Matt was relieved. "I think that Cruise, International stands for Cruz, and that the international part has to do with the way they move drugs from South America. Chico told us about it."

137

"Think he's involved?"

"Chico? No way! Oh, gosh, what's going to happen to him if his brothers are arrested?"

"Nothing's ever simple, Matt."

"Don't you think we ought to report it?"

"Let me think on it for a couple of days. Don't say anything to Chico."

"You're all fueled, Stratford," the FBO operator called out.

Tom stepped to the counter and handed his credit card to the operator. He signed the receipt and shoved a copy into his pocket, motioning for Matt to follow him. Within minutes they were in the air for Teterboro.

Van Ryck was pacing the ramp when Tom taxied the 310 to the end of the row of Cessnas. "How's your fuel, Stratford?"

"What's up?"

"My guy in Boston got ramped. You'll have to haul his load to Pittsburgh."

"It's not overweight, it is? I don't want to get stuck in Pittsburgh."

"The weight's fine. It was his physical. He's two weeks overdue." Van Ryck swore. "I wish those bureaucrats had to do the flying. They might be a little more sympathetic."

Matt and Tom loaded the plane rapidly and lifted off for Logan. Matt slept most of the way to Boston. It was 2:30 by the time they loaded the mail sacks in Boston. "You want to take it up?" Tom asked.

Matt shook his head. "I'm beat. How do you do this every night?"

"I've been flying so long, I could probably do it in my sleep. It's the price you pay to be a night pilot."

"How come you're flying freight, Tom? You're a great instructor."

"Thanks, Matt. I haven't done any instructing in years. Used to do a lot of it, when I was in Princeton, and for a while after.

It got so I didn't like the responsibility of another person with me.

"If you have a car wreck, everybody's sorry. If you have a plane crash, even your friends figure it must have been your fault. I didn't want to chance it anymore."

"How come you're teaching me?"

"I don't know. It just felt right. I haven't taught anyone to fly since my wife."

"Did she like flying?"

"Sure. She grew up around planes. Her dad was a Flying Farmer, had a strip on his place in eastern Oregon. That's how I met her. I was on my mission out there, and her dad was the district president.

"I went back to visit after my mission, met LeeAnn when she came home from school. We got married at the end of the summer, and I took her to Princeton with me. We were there four years, had a little boy. We wanted more, but it didn't happen."

"My mom and dad lost two kids, Mark and Luke."

"That's tough, Matt."

"My dad was gone both times. They thought she'd lose John, but he was born after Dad was killed. I can remember the day Dad left. Mom asked him not to go. She said she didn't think she could stand to lose another baby with him gone, but he went anyway. He never looked back."

"You've never forgiven him, have you?"

"I'm not sure how I feel. When I was little, I just accepted that he had to go, but now I know he wanted to. What would you have done?"

"I don't know. People are different. With LeeAnn, having a baby got to be awful important. When she didn't get pregnant again, she was real torn up. All our friends were having their second and third kids. That's when I taught her to fly. I thought it would take her mind off having a baby. After I got my master's,

I took a job on the West Coast. We were based in Seattle. We'd rent a plane and fly down to see her folks."

Tom checked his dials and flicked his mike for a weather report.

"I thought courier pilots didn't bother with weather reports," Matt teased.

"We don't let them stop us, but you've seen how much weather affects us. Weather's like life — you make allowances for it, but you still have to keep on flying."

"So you went to Seattle. Was that when you flew for the airline?"

"Yep. I liked it, and LeeAnn was glad to be back west. Then she got pregnant again. We went up to British Columbia for a week's vacation, took Tommy with us, to celebrate. We were on our way down to her folks to tell them the news."

Tom paused for a long moment, then swallowed. "I hated the strip on the farm. It was too short, and it lay crossways to the prevailing winds. There was a steep hill at the end. I told Don, LeeAnn's dad, a dozen times to move the darned thing. But it ran between two fields, and he didn't want to change the fences."

Tom paused again. "I wanted to land in Baker and rent a car, but LeeAnn talked me out of it. She was tired, we'd been flying a long time, and she wanted to get home to her folks. She had a couple of hundred hours flying time, just enough to be overconfident. She couldn't see why I was worried. Tommy was five by then, but sometimes he'd wake up crying with bad dreams. He woke up and began crying, so LeeAnn took him up front on her lap.

"I touched down, and a gust of wind flipped the plane into the alfalfa field. We hit a wheel on the center pivot sprinkler going about sixty. The pipe smashed right through the cockpit. LeeAnn and Tommy were both killed. It was years before I quit wishing I'd been killed too."

140

Tom took out a handkerchief and blew his nose. "After I got out of the hospital, I didn't want to fly, so I took a job teaching in Seattle. We had too many friends there, so I moved to L.A. After a couple of years, I started flying again, but I've never stayed in one place too long. Sooner or later, people start asking questions.

" 'Why' is the first thing people want to know. They feel safer if they can figure out why something happened. So many people think that plane crashes are always the pilot's fault. I got tired of explaining. If I was to blame at all, it wasn't my flying, it was not landing in Baker. Don't let anybody talk you out of doing what you feel you should do, Matt. Then no matter what happens, you'll know you did the right thing."

"Did your wife's parents blame you?"

"You know, they didn't. They held me together through the whole thing. Don never did move that strip. I finally gave up trying to get him to. Funny thing, he was killed during takeoff about five years ago. He didn't get enough lift, slammed into the hill. That's when Ruth, LeeAnn's mother, gave me the picture of the wild geese."

"The one you gave Mom?"

"Yeah. I thought she ought to have it. She's got flying in her soul too. Most pilots' wives do. They may not even like flying, but they understand that old wild goose. They can let us fly, knowing we always come back."

"Dad didn't."

"He could have been just as dead from a heart attack or a car wreck. It wasn't the flying that took him. That's why your mom lets you fly with me."

"If it wasn't flying, what was it?"

"We're back to 'why' again. I don't know why some people die before others do, Matt. But Heavenly Father knows what he's doing. I can't let the things I don't understand make me doubt the things I know are true."

141

"Mom says the right question isn't 'why,' it's 'what.' "

"That's what we're all trying to figure out. What do we do next?"

"Have you got it figured out yet, Tom?"

"When I do, I'll let you know." Tom keyed the mike. "Flying Dutchman 2407, requesting permission to land."

The tower brought them in on the middle runway. They unloaded the mail sacks, and Matt followed Tom into the FBO.

The operator looked up. "We're out of fuel, if that's what you're after. Sorry. The storm's run us ragged tonight."

"Anyplace else we can get fuel?"

"You can hop over to Allegheny County Airport. They've got fuel—I just checked."

"Thanks."

They walked back to the waiting 310. There was no cargo for Harrisburg.

"You awake enough now to take us off?"

"Sure, Tom."

Matt handled the takeoff while Tom managed the radios. From Pittsburgh, the flight was just a hop up and then down to the county airport.

"You'll be landing on your own soon," Tom promised as they put the plane down. "You're already right down to the flare."

A sleepy FBO operator refueled the plane, filled out the paper work, and wished them luck on their flight home. Matt did the takeoff unassisted again.

"Terrific, Matt!" Tom yawned. "Boy! I'm beat to death, and my head's killing me. When we're on course, I'll rest my eyes for a few minutes."

When Matt reached altitude, Tom leaned back and closed his eyes. Matt flew alone through the dark, checking and re-checking his gauges. What would he do if something went wrong? He looked at the sleeping pilot. The next twenty minutes seemed like forever. Tom sat up with a start, then relaxed. He checked their position. "You did a great job, Matt. Thanks for the rest."

"You want to sleep some more?"

"This will do me until we get home. I'll crash most of the day."

"So will I."

"I'll pick up you and John at 3:30. I promised him last night we'd take him to the airport and let him sit in the plane."

Matt got up his nerve. "Does Mom know about your wife?"

"Sure does. First person I've ever told who didn't ask me. We got to talking one day at the mall, and it just came out."

"What'd she say?"

"She gave me the best advice anybody ever did. She told me the 'if onlies' would kill me if I let them. You know, 'If only I'd done this, or that.' You can't go back, you have to go on. Putting the 'if onlies' out of the way may be the hardest thing I've done since the crash, but I've got a feeling that she's right."

Tom rubbed his forehead.

"Shouldn't you do something about that headache?"

"It'll probably go away when I get some sleep. It's been a long night."

Matt's mind was busy with all the unexpected information he'd been given. Neither spoke during the hour it took to reach Harrisburg. Finally, they dropped through the cloud cover. The runway lights beckoned them in. The 310 nudged the runway in a feather-light landing. "Take her in, Matt," Tom said, as he leaned back in his seat and closed his eyes, leaving Matt to handle the controls.

Matt struggled to remember everything. He carefully followed radioed instructions, working the craft around the building into their usual parking place. Light was just breaking in the east.

Tom hadn't awakened, so Matt shook him lightly by the shoulder. "Hey, we're here."

"What? Oh, good job, Matt. Thanks." Tom struggled with his seatbelt, opened the door, and climbed out. He missed his step and stumbled against the tail. Matt scrambled down and grabbed the older man.

"I'm okay now, but my headache's back. Can you drive the truck?"

"Sure." Matt climbed behind the wheel and drove to Tom's apartment. "I'll bring the truck over later," he said as Tom climbed out.

15

Wʜᴇɴ Mᴀᴛᴛ's ᴍᴏᴛʜᴇʀ ᴡᴏᴋᴇ ʜɪᴍ ᴀᴛ 1:30 ɪɴ ᴛʜᴇ ᴀꜰᴛᴇʀɴᴏᴏɴ, he felt as though he'd barely fallen asleep.

"I'm sorry to wake you, but if John's going with Brother Stratford to the airport, I'll have to leave him home with you."

"It's okay, Mom. I'm going with them. If we go, that is. Tom had an awful bad headache last night."

"He's had a couple lately. I wonder whether he has migraines."

"He told Morrison—that's the pilot from Toronto—that he thought it was flu last week, but I don't see how it could be flu again. He ought to get it checked out."

"Maybe he was just tired; you had a pretty long night."

"We sure did. I flew the plane alone for about twenty minutes."

"How'd it go?"

"It went fine. I wonder what it'd be like to fly in the daytime?"

"Brother Stratford said he wanted to take you to the airport over Christmas vacation to let you try some daytime flying."

"Don't you mind, Mom?"

"You know, I don't; it seems natural. I'm not worried when you're with Tom."

"Brother Stratford, Mom."

Matt's mother laughed. "I guess he's Tom to us both."

"He told me about his wife last night."

"I don't think he tells many people."

145

"He said you were the only person he'd told who hadn't asked him first. He said you gave him the best advice he'd ever had."

"Did he really?" Matt's mother smiled. "Well, I'm glad to know I could help. He's helped me enough lately."

John came into the room. "Hey, Matt, I'm going to see your plane today."

"Tom will call us when he gets up. I've got his truck. Only thing, he had a real bad headache last night. He might not want to go today."

"We'll go. Tom promised."

Matt showered and dressed. He straightened up his room while he waited for Tom's call. He put the dirty clothes in the bathroom hamper. The bathroom was a mess too. He found himself getting the Fantastic and the sponge from under the sink.

"What're you doing?" John asked, half-eaten apple in hand.

"My chores. You got yours done?"

"Course not."

"Well, then, get in there and get started. You dust, and I'll vacuum when I get done with my room."

Matt quickly finished the bathroom he and John shared, then returned to his room. The half-finished model lay scattered on the desk. He'd just leave it until Christmas vacation. He pulled the vacuum out of the hall closet, plugged the cord into the hall socket, and ran it into his room. He pushed it around quickly, then went down the hall into John's room. John lay on his bed, looking at a Superman comic.

"I told you I'd vacuum your room if you got it ready. How come you're not done?"

"I was working on it, honest. Then I found this comic under the bed."

"What else have you got under there?"

"Not much. Do you want me to look?"

146

"Of course, Dummy! I can't vacuum if there's junk all over the floor. Come on, Tom'll be calling any time."

"Do I have to?"

"You sure do. It'll be a nice surprise for Mom if she comes home while we're gone and we've cleaned up our stuff."

John put the vacuum away after Matt finished. Matt mixed up grape juice and made tuna sandwiches. Just as they finished eating, the phone rang.

"Matt here."

"This is Tom. You guys about ready to go?"

"Sure. When should I pick you up?"

"Give me half an hour to grab a bite."

"Okay, Tom, see you in a few."

Matt finished his second sandwich and put the dishes in the sink. Heck, it wouldn't take fifteen minutes to get to Tom's. "Come on, John. You rinse. Then we'll head for Tom's."

Just as they pulled on their coats, the doorbell rang. Chico Cruz stood there, breath frosting the air. "I have to talk to you, Matt."

"Golly, Chico, I was just walking out the door. I'm picking Tom up. We're going to the airport to show my brother the plane."

Chico's face fell.

"Let me give Tom a call. I don't think he'd mind if you came along."

Matt dialed Tom's number, but there was no answer.

"He probably walked down to Wendy's to get something to eat. Why don't you come with us? I'd like you to meet Tom anyway."

Chico stood silent, a frown on his face. It cleared. "Thanks, I'll come."

They crowded into the cab of the little truck, John sitting between the two seats. "Gosh," Matt said, "I forgot how small this truck is."

"Chico and I can sit in the back after we get Tom," John said.

"That's fine," Chico agreed. "The sleeper will keep the wind off."

Matt hopped out at Tom's apartment, while John and Chico climbed inside the cap. Tom was just putting dishes in the sink.

"I tried to call you," Matt said, moving a pile of magazines off the couch to sit down. "You didn't answer, so I figured you'd gone down to Wendy's."

"I was in the shower. Time I got out, the phone had quit. What's up?"

"Chico Cruz, the Cuban kid I told you about, came by. When I told him we were leaving, he acted kind of funny. He's usually cool. I think something's wrong, so I brought him along."

"This is the kid with the Marielito brothers, right?"

"Yeah."

"Well, maybe we can find out what's bugging him. Let's go." He picked up his jacket from the chair, then turned to lock the door. "I hate living where you have to lock everything up. Used to be, we never locked doors."

They drove in silence down the street. Tom wheeled the truck onto the turnpike. John opened the window between the cab and the cap.

"Shut the window, John."

"It's cold back here."

"How you guys making it?" Tom asked Chico.

"Fine." He reached for John. "You'll be warmer if you zip your coat and put on your hood."

John fumbled with the zipper. Finally, he got it started, ran the zipper up, and pulled his hood over his head. Chico tied it for him.

Minutes later they were through the airport gate.

"I wanna see the plane first," John said, running ahead of

148

the group. He turned around, skipping backwards. "Please, Tom, can we see the plane?"

"Why not?"

"This one's ours," Matt said as they approached the Cessna 310.

Tom boosted John through the cargo door. "Hop in the left seat. Climb up there with him, Matt, and show your brother how to be a pilot."

Matt climbed up the wing and settled himself in the right seat. Soon John was making engine noises and holding the mike in his hand.

Tom and Chico were getting acquainted. A tall, thin man, well bundled against the cold, cut across the ramp toward them. It was Dr. Samuels. "Hi, Stewart," Tom said, sticking out his hand.

The math instructor shook it. "Good afternoon, Tom." He nodded to the Cuban, "Hello, Mr. Cruz."

"Stay here a minute, John, and don't fiddle with anything! That's Dr. Samuels, my math teacher." Matt hopped down from the wing.

"You know Matt Hansen," Tom said. "He's my Friday night co-pilot. Does a good job for me."

"I know both these young men. They're going to win the district math competition in February."

"I hope you're right, Dr. Samuels," Chico said.

"I will be, if Miss Satterfield cooperates."

"I think she will," Matt said. "Her mother works for mine. I told her Chico's dad was a famous mathematician. I figured she'd tell Laura."

"You didn't!" Chico said.

"I sure did. After all, we're doing this for him."

A slow smile lightened Chico's face. "We are?"

"Sure. We're a team, aren't we?"

"How was the flying today, Stewart?"

149

"Good enough. Fortunately, last night's storm had passed. My Cessna 180 doesn't have the electronic gadgetry Tom's plane does. I'm a fair-weather pilot."

Matt asked, "Do you fly a lot, Dr. Samuels?"

"Every week. It's the light in my darkness. Are you learning to fly, Mr. Cruz?"

"No, Dr. Samuels. I came with Matt. Flying is expensive."

"You're right. I didn't buy my 180 with my school-teacher's salary, but there are always opportunities, if you look for them."

"That's what my brother Alfredo says, but I don't agree with him. Some opportunities should be left alone."

Something in Chico's tone caught Matt's attention. Tom appeared relaxed, but he was studying Chico. Tom looked at Matt and shook his head slightly.

"Tell you what, Stewart," Tom said, "We're having a family Christmas party next Saturday night at our church: turkey dinner and a Santa for the kids. Why don't you and your wife come with me?"

"Hey, Chico, why don't you come too," Matt said. "Cindi'll be there, and one or two other kids you know. Maybe Beef'll come."

"I'd like that, Matt."

"I'll ask Marsha," Dr. Samuels told Tom. "If Michael is well, she might enjoy going."

"How's he doing?"

"Winter's always the worst time for respiratory problems."

"Check with Marsha and give me a call."

"I'll do that," Dr. Samuels said with his thin smile.

"Hey, Matt," John called through the cockpit window. "How do I get down?"

"I'll rescue you," Tom said. He opened the cargo door and lifted the little boy down. "You'll make a pilot, too, I'll bet." Tom climbed up the wing. "Come on up, Chico, and I'll give you the dime tour."

"Would you like to see my 180?"

"We sure would!" Matt and John followed Dr. Samuels across the ramp to inspect his plane. When they returned, Chico and Tom were standing by the 310, still talking. "Matt, you take the back with John. Chico and I'll ride up front."

Matt crawled in over the tailgate. A hearty twinge from his leg reminded him that he couldn't do the things he used to. Tom boosted John up and slammed the sleeper window.

They dropped Chico at the apartment he shared with his brothers. It was at least an hour's walk from Matt's house. As Chico jogged up the walk, Matt realized he still didn't know why Chico had come to his house.

"Climb up front," Tom said. "You can sit in the middle, John."

Matt saw the wrinkles between Tom's eyes deepen.

"How's your headache?"

"Just hangs in there, reminding me it might start up again."

"Why don't you get it checked?"

"If anything were wrong, it would have shown up on my physical. I'll be all right. I'll get some dinner and turn in."

He swung the truck into the circular driveway. "Tell your mom I said 'hi.' "

"Thanks, Tom. Will do." He poked his little brother.

"Thanks, Tom," John said.

16

BEEF WAS AS PROMPT AS HE'D BEEN LAST SUNDAY MORNING. LaMar and Cindi met them in the foyer, and they went to opening exercises together. Beef seemed at ease as they sat in class. Matt envied him his easy confidence. He watched him closely. Beef was an actor. He wondered if some of that confidence was assumed. Whatever it was, Matt wished he had it too.

As Sister Goodman's class discussed commitment to the gospel, the issue of persecution arose. Sister Goodman read Colonel Thomas Kane's description of the Saints being driven from Nauvoo, which he had presented before the Pennsylvania Historical Society in 1850.

Beef was dubious. "Did this really happen? I thought we had religious freedom in America."

"Oh, yes, it happened," Sister Goodman responded. "My great-great-grandfather MacRae's family were driven out of Nauvoo. He was in Liberty jail with the Prophet Joseph when twenty thousand Saints were driven out of Missouri the winter of 1838–39."

Several students interjected family stories of persecutions. LaMar Norton's family had been handcart pioneers.

"I never heard about this," Beef said. "How come our U.S. history books don't tell us about it?"

"They don't mention hanging Quakers on Boston Common, either," Jennifer said. "My family was driven out of Massachusetts for being Quakers."

John Hestletine, a young man in his late twenties, was the

sacrament meeting speaker. When he mentioned going to Bloomsburg on a football scholarship, Beef and Matt both perked up their ears. Brother Hestletine told of his conversion and his mission in Florida. It had been tough on him, coming as he had from a family where everybody had done his own thing and nobody had followed rules.

"My mission president almost gave up on me," he said, "but he could see that I really did have a testimony. So he kept working on me. My companions worked on me too." Several returned missionaries in the congregation laughed.

"I met Jeannie at BYU. All her family live in Utah, but here we are in Pennsylvania, where I'm from. We hope to teach the gospel to my family, but they're a hard-headed bunch."

As they left the chapel, Beef turned to Matt. "I thought you had to be born a Mormon."

"Gosh, no. Probably most of the people at church are converts."

"Man, I think I could go for a church where you can laugh. My dad would never believe it. Which reminds me, we've got our family reunion over Christmas. We're leaving Friday right after school. Will you tell your mom I'm sorry I can't work this weekend? I forgot all about the reunion when I told her I'd work."

"No problem," Matt said. "I'll tell her. I can be Santa."

Beef punched him lightly in the shoulder. As they turned to leave, Bishop Adams crossed the foyer. "Matt, could you go home teaching about three?"

"Sure."

"What's home teaching?" Beef asked as the two climbed into his car.

Matt explained, but while Mrs. Satterfield had been politely skeptical, Beef was interested. "You mean someone visits every family in your church each month?"

"Well, they're supposed to."

"Who do you visit?"

"The family with the little girl in the wheelchair is one family. I don't know who the other one is."

"What do you do when you visit?"

"We talk awhile, usually give a lesson, see if they need help. That's how I met Tom Stratford."

"I thought you guys were friends."

"We sure are. But I'd probably never have gotten to know him if he wasn't our home teacher." Matt climbed out of the sports car. "Later."

Beef grinned and gunned the car a little, flipping gravel as he spun out of the driveway.

Matt's mother was working at the sink when he came in. "How about having dinner around two?"

"Sounds good, Mom. I'm going home teaching with the bishop at three."

"Do you think you'll be back by five or five-thirty? I've got to teach the temple preparation class at six."

"I think so. We have only two families. What's your lesson about?"

"Keeping the commandments. People need to know what they're getting into when they go to the temple."

"What are we having for dinner?"

"Meatloaf and potatoes au gratin. Tom's coming."

"Potatoes all rotten?" John asked from the doorway.

"Yep," said Matt. "With cheese all over them."

"Matt, stop teasing John. Potatoes au gratin means with a cheese sauce."

"Can I grate the cheese, Mom, please?"

"Get the cheese from the fridge, and I'll find you the grater and a bowl. Would you peel the potatoes, Matt?"

"Tom's been around a lot lately, hasn't he, Mom?" Matt commented as they worked.

"I wouldn't say it's anything out of the ordinary. He's going with me to the temple preparation class, that's all."

Tom and the Hansens were still sitting around the table when Bishop Adams knocked. "Let me run up and get my coat," Matt said.

"How's the Santa business, Sister Hansen?"

"It's more work than I thought it would be. I had no idea how hard it is to manage employees."

"There's quite a difference between hourly employees and self-starters who get involved in network marketing."

"I'm finding that out. Only a few of my Santa's helpers have any initiative. Sometimes I feel like I'm pushing a string uphill."

"In the rain," the bishop added. "How're Matt's flying lessons coming, Tom?"

"He'll make a pilot. It's kind of nice to have company in the cockpit again. Been a long time."

The bishop smiled. "It's a relief to see Matt alive again."

"Matt's a lot stronger than he realizes, Bishop. He's a darned good kid."

"He's not nearly as stubborn as he used to be," Nancy added.

"We're off," the bishop said as Matt came downstairs.

The first family they visited were the Joneses. Sister Jones was Relief Society president. Their five children ranged from Jennifer, who was in Matt's Sunday School class, down to Jeanette, who was eight, with three boys in between.

After the bishop had given the lesson, the boys drifted off. Jennifer wheeled Jeanette down the hall. "How're you two doing?" Bishop Adams asked.

"We're still hanging in there," the father replied. "But I'd be lying to you if I said it was easy."

"Your family has one of the most difficult challenges I know."

Sister Jones nodded. "Bishop Adams, sometimes I'm so

tired I don't think I can go on. When I hear sisters complain about changing baby diapers, I want to scream. I've been changing diapers for eight years, and I'll be doing it the rest of Jeanette's life."

Matt stirred. "Sister Jones, why is Jeanette in a wheelchair?"

"It's a birth defect called spina bifida. Part of her spine isn't formed correctly, so she doesn't have control over the lower part of her body. Lots of spina bifida children learn to walk, but others are mentally retarded. Jeanette does so many things that the doctors never thought she'd do, so we hope for a lot."

"You've had to go by faith," Bishop Adams said, "and that's the hardest thing in the world."

"Not for me," Sister Jones contradicted. "The hardest thing is the ridiculous things people say to me. Someone told me once that having a handicapped child would teach me to be more loving. I could have hit her! If one more person tells me what a blessing having a handicapped child is, I may offer to lend them Jeanette."

"People don't realize the price you pay for that blessing," Bishop Adams said.

"It is a blessing, Bishop. But often that isn't much comfort. After Jeanette was born, I really needed comfort. I didn't need preaching; I understood the gospel."

Matt was interested. "Wasn't there anything that helped?"

"Oh, yes." Sister Jones laughed. "Well, I can laugh about it now, but at the time it wasn't funny. I had a visiting teacher who worked with handicapped kids. She'd listen to everything I had to say, then she'd say, 'Linda, how did Jeanette do today?'

" 'Today?' I'd say. 'She did good.'

" 'That's all you can afford to think about,' she'd reply. 'Just remember that she did good today.'

"She was tough with me, she was so upfront. She didn't minimize the problems we'd have, but she helped me learn to take one day at a time. After a while, I could look at the whole picture. It's true, Jeanette has been a great blessing to our whole family. When we give a lot of love, we can't help but grow. But we don't need people telling us that."

"You sure don't!" Brother Jones said emphatically. "You can't imagine how many people told us Jeannette was handicapped because we were so good or because we had such a loving family. I was mad at the Lord over that for about four years. If Jeannette's handicap was the reward for my being good, I wished I hadn't been so darn good.

"It took me a long time to get over. When I meet a family that's just had a handicapped child, I tell them it's natural to feel angry. It's letting the anger get out of hand that's a problem. There's a whole grieving process to go through."

Bishop Adams agreed. "I see the same thing with people who've been widowed or divorced. They have to deal with a lot of guilt and anger before they go on. If they bury it, it just festers. You have to come to terms with what might have been if only things were different."

"I know what you mean," Matt said. "All fall I kept thinking 'if only I hadn't hurt my leg.' It didn't do a bit of good."

"Exactly," Sister Jones agreed. "They're still trying to find out what causes spina bifida. I kept thinking for a long time 'if only I'd done this or that.' Finally, I realized that Jeanette's handicap wasn't caused by anything we had done. She's Heavenly Father's child too. And he loves her. With his help, we can learn to handle whatever trials he gives us. But every once in a while I still think 'if only'."

"What was the most helpful thing someone said to you?" the bishop asked Brother Jones.

"You know, it was a friend up in Michigan, not even a member of the Church. When I told him about Jeanette, he just said, 'Oh, Brian, I'm so sorry.'"

"I'll remember that," Bishop Adams said. "Sometimes what

157

we think will comfort people denies them their feelings, or even belittles their problem."

Matt remembered how many times he'd said, "It's not the end of the world," when one of his friends had a problem. He vowed never to say it again.

"We'd better be on our way," the bishop said. "We'll see you at the Christmas party."

"Thanks for coming," Sister Jones said.

The bishop sighed as he started the car. "I used to ask the Lord to lighten our burdens, Matt. Now I just ask him to strengthen our backs."

"Man! I thought I had troubles. Maybe I can't play football, but Jeanette can't even walk."

"Everybody's handicapped, Matt, one way or another. Some people are spiritually handicapped. That's worse because it lasts forever. The Joneses are really doing well. It will always be hard for them, but they haven't let themselves become bitter, and the gospel gives them hope. Parents of handicapped children look forward to the resurrection with more anticipation and joy than the rest of us."

He swung the car up the ramp onto the expressway. "You've never met the Miners. He used to be a bishop in Williamsport, but they haven't been active in quite a few years."

"How could a bishop go inactive?"

"The same way anybody else does, Matt."

They dropped down off the bypass, turned right, and went down the hill into a subdivision. Less than a minute later, Bishop Adams rang the doorbell. After a long wait, a plump, gray-haired lady opened the door. She didn't smile, but she did step back.

"Come in, Bishop. Henry's in the living room." A small-built man arose from a wing chair. His face was well-lined, and not happily.

158

"Just wanted to drop by and see how things are going. This is Matt Hansen. He's my new companion."

"Matt Hansen? You the football player?"

"Not anymore, I'm afraid."

"Leg injury?"

"Yes, sir."

"Tough on you."

Bishop Adams began talking quietly with Sister Miner. Matt shifted his weight and cleared his throat. "Do you work at the Navy Depot, Brother Miner?"

"No, I'm retired. I've got a workshop downstairs, and I putter."

The bishop looked up. "Don't let him kid you, Matt. He's one of the best miniature craftsmen on the East Coast."

"Miniature craftsman?"

"I make scale model houses, furniture, things like that," Brother Miner said, a flicker of life in his eyes. "I'm working on a 1790 Philadelphia row house now. Would you like to see it?"

"I sure would. I build model planes."

"You might enjoy seeing my houses then." The old man led Matt downstairs.

Matt's eyes widened when he saw the house Brother Miner was building. It was a small but exact replica of the tall, narrow town houses of Colonial Philadelphia. Only one room wide, a staircase climbed from floor to floor. The dining room had a miniature mural painted on the walls. Tiny mahogany furniture decorated the rooms.

"I do the furniture, the house construction, and electricity," Brother Miner explained. "My wife does the rugs, the curtains, and the upholstery. We buy a few things, like dishes."

"What do you do with them after you're finished?"

"Sell them, of course. I've made twenty or twenty-five over the years. Wouldn't have room for them all, even if I could afford to keep them. This row house was written up in *Nutshell*

159

News. It's going to New York to a show." He caressed the roof tiles lightly.

"I bet they cost a fortune to build."

"They do. But I like the building best, so I don't mind building and selling. Other people would rather buy. This Victorian over here is a commission job."

They walked across the room. The extreme attention to detail fascinated Matt. He inspected the gingerbread trim, the velvet-covered carved furniture.

"These must take a ton of time."

"About four months on this one so far. Some of the furniture was already made. It'll bring twenty-five thousand dollars."

"Wow! Who has that kind of money?"

"You'd be surprised at the rich people who enjoy having a little world they can control. It's better than their real one, I guess. Well, I can understand that. After all, illusions beat reality all hollow." Bitterness crept into his voice.

"Where do you get your tools?" Matt asked quickly.

They walked across the room to the workbench. "Dremel makes a good line. I've made some too. If I can't buy what I need, I figure something out."

"I had no idea anybody made things like this."

"How long have you been making models?"

"I made a bunch when I was a kid, before my dad died. But I didn't start to really get into it until I had surgery on my leg. Bishop Adams gave me my first one."

"He's a good man. Too bad everybody in the church isn't like him. Let's go upstairs."

When they returned to the living room, the bishop was standing near Sister Miner's chair. She looked as if she'd been crying, but she smiled at Matt.

"Ready to go, Matt? Now, remember, we'd love to see you at the Christmas party Saturday night."

"Bishop," Sister Miner protested, "I just can't stand all the families."

"There's no need for you to feel that way."

"All those talks. Never give up; accept your children; love them for what they are." She began to cry.

The bishop motioned Matt into a chair, while he sat down on the couch facing Sister Miner. "No one who tried as hard as you and Bishop Miner did to teach your son correct principles could love him for what he is. God doesn't expect you to. Loving people for what they are when they're wicked is impossible. We love them for *who* they are. They're children of our Heavenly Father, all of them. We love them, but if we can't distance ourselves from them when they've committed themselves to a path of evil, we'd lose our minds."

"It was so ugly, Bishop Adams. Yet at every conference I was being told to be a loving mother. How could I?"

"You are a loving mother. An unloving mother doesn't care what her children do. You know you did the best you could, and that's all the Lord expects of anyone."

"I wish the members understood that," Brother Miner interjected, "instead of being so sure it's the parents' fault when a kid goes wrong."

Matt wanted very much to ask what they were talking about. But he sensed he should keep quiet.

"I've seen the same thing," Bishop Adams was saying. "But you and I have had those parents in our offices, and you know the difference as well as I do."

"Well," Brother Miner said emphatically, "I'm not giving anyone else a chance to wonder what we did wrong. I've had all of that I could stand."

"I can't blame you," the bishop replied. "But remember, the Lord knows you did the best you could. That's what makes you successful parents, not how your kids turn out. He had

161

quite a time with a third of his, and we don't think less of him for it. Don't forget that we'd love to have you with us."

Bishop Adams and Matt stood up to leave. A few moments later, as the bishop backed his car from the driveway, Matt asked, "What did their son do?"

"You don't need to know," the bishop answered firmly but kindly. "He's serving twenty-five years at White Hill."

"Twenty-five years! It must have been awful."

"It was."

"But how could such a nice couple have a son like that?"

"That's the attitude that drove Brother Miner into inactivity, Matt. When tough things happen, people try to figure out why. In trying to do that, they can make some pretty unrighteous judgments. I wonder whether they realize that, with some spirits, the parents have done better than anyone else could have."

"It sure must be hard to live with, though."

"Everybody has hard things to deal with in life."

"I guess it's how you deal with them that makes the difference," Matt said.

17

WHEN MATT OPENED THE KITCHEN DOOR MONDAY AFTERNOON, he saw the note on the refrigerator: "The car's at Reynolds'. They promised to have it inspected by four. Pick me up at the mall. Mrs. Bare will keep John until we get home. Love, Mom."

Before he walked to the service station, a mile down the road, he decided to check on the car. "Matt Hansen here, Bert. The car ready?"

"You can pick it up any time."

"I'll be right down."

Matt walked quickly through the early winter dusk. Heavy gray clouds hung low in the north. Piles of snow lined the roadside, forcing Matt to walk in the narrow roadway. Cars came uncomfortably close. Matt was glad to turn into the service station. He pushed open the door into the office.

"I'll send your mom the bill. She should check those brakes in a couple of months; they're getting close."

"Thanks, Bert. I'll tell her."

Matt threaded the car through the heavy commuter traffic to the mall. He parked in the employee parking and entered the mall through Hess's.

The booth was crowded with parents bringing children for pictures after work. Matt's mother was running the camera while Mrs. Satterfield took money. Tom was playing Santa, a pair of black preschoolers on his lap. As they smiled, Matt's mom snapped the picture.

"How cute!" she said as she mounted the photo in the

cardboard holder. Nancy took the keys from Matt's outstretched hand.

"The car passed inspection, but Bert said to keep an eye on the brakes. He thinks you should check them again in a couple of months. The shoes are beginning to wear."

"At least I won't have to worry about it until after Christmas."

Mr. Rawlins approached the booth. He hesitated when he saw the crowd.

"Take over the camera, Matt. I want to find out what Mr. Rawlins heard about his tests."

They walked across the hallway. Nancy perched on the edge of the covered fountain. Though Matt could see them talking, he couldn't hear them.

There was a lull in the crowd. Tom stepped down from the Santa chair and put up his "Santa is feeding his reindeer" sign. "How you doing, Matt?"

"Great!"

"I'll go get out of this suit. Ask your mom if she'd like to get dinner."

While Mr. Rawlins followed Tom to the dressing rooms, Matt did.

"I don't think we'd better. John would feel left out."

"Gosh, Mom, he thinks he should do everything with us. What's he expect?"

"Maybe he expects a little time with me," Nancy answered tartly. "You got plenty of it when you were young."

Tom returned. "How about it, Nan?"

"I think I'd better collect my other son."

Tom shrugged his shoulders. "Whatever you say. See you tomorrow." The pilot turned and walked briskly down the crowded mall.

"Is he mad, Mom?"

"Oh, Matt, I don't know! Right now I've got other things

164

to worry about. Let me talk to Mr. Rawlins for a minute, then we'll go home."

Mr. Rawlins came back with his Santa suit on.

"Now, you're sure you feel up to this?"

"I don't feel no worse than I've been feeling."

"Do you have everything you need at home?"

"I'm just fine. There's kerosene in the can and food in the refrigerator. If my old car wasn't on the blink, I wouldn't rightly have a thing to complain about."

"Well, you call if you need anything."

"You've already done plenty, Missus Hansen."

Matt and Nancy walked across the mall. "I still think we should have gone with Tom."

"That's enough, Matt. I told you I wanted to go home."

The next morning, Nancy was preoccupied as she put breakfast on the table.

"What's the matter, Mom?"

"I'm just worried. I'll get over it." Nancy turned inward when she worried. She also became a little sharp, so Matt decided to drop the subject. She usually told him when she'd worked through things. He wondered whether she was afraid that Tom was angry with her.

Matt and Chico were early for activity period. They talked planes with Dr. Samuels until Laura came. She smiled at them both and took a seat between Matt and Chico. The session went much like the preceding one: Dr. Samuels threw out problems and they struggled to work them quickly. Chico completed an extremely difficult problem far ahead of both Matt and Laura.

"That's great!" Laura said.

Dr. Samuels looked faintly pleased. "I believe we have a team." Matt gave Chico a thumbs-up sign.

Matt was still feeling pleased when he got off the bus. He found his mother sitting at the kitchen table. Matt could tell she'd been crying. "Mom, what's wrong?"

165

She motioned to the newspaper on the table. Matt picked it up. "Man killed in hit-and-run accident," the headline read. "Harold Rawlins, 67, of Lisburn, was killed last night in a hit-and-run accident while crossing Lisburn Rd. near Capitol Plaza Mall. Police arrested Eric Rasmussen, 21, of Camp Hill, near the scene. Rasmussen was charged with driving under the influence, possession of narcotics, and leaving the scene of an accident."

Matt sat down slowly.

"He was trying so hard. Just as he was finally beginning to succeed, he . . . " Tears welled up, and Nancy started to cry again.

Matt realized how much he'd begun to like the old man. Maybe he had made a mess of his life, but there was something pathetic about his determination to give something to his granddaughters.

"Oh gosh, Mom, the money!"

"What money?"

"In the silverware drawer. What if somebody finds it and keeps it?"

"My word, Matt, you're right! We'd better go over there and see about it. I've still got his key. We can find his son's address in Baltimore and send the money to him. You drive," she said, digging the keys from her purse and handing them to Matt.

"Where's John?"

"Tom took him to the mall. He's going to see whether Beef can come in and substitute. He'll bring John home when Beef gets there."

"I thought maybe Tom was mad at you."

"I don't think so, Matt. Tom's a rare person. He's not laid back because he doesn't care; he's laid back because he believes people usually have good reasons for the things they do. Since he doesn't let them bother him much, he's easy to be around."

"He sure manages to be around when we need him."

"Yes, he does. You wouldn't think he notices as much as he does, but he's pretty much on the ball."

The car wound its way along the country road. Matt turned into the narrow lane leading to the junkyard. The car jounced over the ruts in the frozen driveway. Mr. Rawlins's Subaru still rested under the white oak trees near the trailer. A dark-green Nissan Pulsar was parked next to it.

"Uh oh, Mom, I wonder who that is."

"It may be the owner of the yard. Let's go see."

Matt's mother tapped on the door. A slim-built, capable-looking man opened the door.

"I'm Nancy Hansen. Mr. Rawlins worked for me."

The stranger hesitated, then stepped back into the trailer. Matt and his mother followed him.

"I'm Hal Rawlins."

"You must be his son from Baltimore."

"How'd you know?"

"You've got his name. He told me about you."

"Yeah," he said bitterly, "his name's the only thing he ever gave me."

"Mr. Rawlins said you didn't care for him."

"Why should I? I was scared to death of him as a kid. The only memories I have of him are when he was drunk. Then Mom took me back to Baltimore, and we were dirt poor. If he ever gave her a dime, I never knew about it. I had my own way to make, and it's no thanks to either of them that I made it."

"That's what he told me, Mr. Rawlins. He was proud of you, and he loved his grandchildren."

The younger Rawlins snorted. "He never paid a bit of attention to them. Not that I'd have wanted him around, anyway.

167

Look at this place! Who wants his kids to know their grandfather was nothing but a junkyard dog?"

"He was more than that," Matt interrupted.

"Yeah? You tell me what."

"He was a Santa Claus. That's what he did for my mom."

"How'd you ever let that old drunk around kids?"

"Mr. Rawlins gave me his word he'd be sober, and he always was."

"How long did that last—two or three days?"

"Mr. Rawlins, I know you have a lot of reason to feel bitter, but I really do think your father was trying. Maybe I saw him differently, or maybe I just didn't have as much experience with him. I didn't come to argue with you. I just want to help. What have you decided about the funeral?"

"Why have a funeral? My father didn't believe in anything that I know of. None of us are churchgoers. I'll get him buried as soon as I work things out with the police."

"If you'd like, Matt and I could arrange a memorial service for him. Are you going to bury him in Baltimore?"

"He was a vet. They'll bury him at Fort Indiantown Gap."

"That'll be nice."

"At least it's cheap!" He took a step toward the door.

"Shall we arrange the funeral for you?"

"Oh, go ahead, if it means something to you. Call me, and tell me when to come. I'm in the book."

He stepped down from the trailer, then stopped in his tracks. He turned around, struggling for words. "Look, Mrs. Hansen, I don't mean to sound rude, but I just don't have any feeling for my father. And if I don't get out of here, I'll be late for work."

"Don't worry about it. I'll take care of things and give you a call."

"Thanks. If I'm not home, try me at work, Inner Harbor Precinct, Baltimore Police Department, Detective Sergeant

168

Rawlins. They'll know where to find me." He opened his car door. "I really do have to hit the road."

Nancy stood in the doorway watching the taillights bounce up the roadway. She wiped tears from her eyes.

"He doesn't think much of his dad, does he?" Matt said.

"He has his reasons. Even when people change, the consequences of what they were before can last a long time. I don't suppose he'll want his father's things, but let's pack them up in case he does. If not, we can take them to Goodwill later." She found some paper bags under the sink and carried them back to the bedroom.

"What about the kitchen stuff, Mom? Should I leave it here, or put it in a bag?"

"Go ahead and put it . . . Oh, my word, Matt! We forgot the money!"

Matt pulled open the silverware drawer. It was still stuffed full of bills.

"I can't believe it!" She sat down on the worn couch and began to laugh. "Matt, I think I'm losing my mind."

Matt stared at her, then he began to laugh too. The two of them sat in the shabby living room and laughed until tears came. Nancy finally managed to say, "How much money do you suppose is in that drawer?"

Matt crossed the tiny living room and emptied the silverware into a grocery bag. He carried the drawer to the table and began sorting the bills. When he finished counting, $1,720 lay in careful stacks on the table.

"Mr. Rawlins must have been struggling a long time. He didn't save all that working for me. I hope his son realizes that when he gets the money. It took a lot of sacrifice for Mr. Rawlins to get this much together."

In a drawer in the bedroom, Matt found a small stack of papers and envelopes. He put the money into a large manila envelope marked "Department of the Army." A beat-up radio/

tape player stood on the windowsill. Matt put it into a bag with the clothes. When he started to chuck the few tapes in after it, his mother stopped him.

"Let's keep the tapes, Matt. Mr. Rawlins's son might want to see what kind of music his father enjoyed. You can tell a lot about people by what they read and listen to."

Matt's mother stacked the grocery bags neatly on the bed against the wall. Matt put the papers, envelopes, and tapes into another bag. "We'll bring them home with us until the funeral," his mother said.

They locked the trailer behind them. "What about his car?" Matt asked.

"It looks as if it belongs with those over there," she replied, "but I suppose if it runs, it could be sold."

"It probably doesn't. Mr. Rawlins said that it was on the blink last night. I'll bet that's why he was walking."

Matt's mother was silent, thinking over the conversation. "Oh, Matt, you're right. I remember him saying that, just before I told him to call me if he needed anything. How could I have missed it?"

"I did too. And I even wondered how he was getting home, but I never thought to ask him. If only I'd taken him home."

When Matt and his mother pulled into the driveway, they saw Tom's truck. He and John were sitting in the kitchen. Spaghetti boiled on the stove, and the aroma of sauce filled the kitchen.

"Hey, Mom, Tom can cook too."

"Well, I can open a jar of Ragu, anyway," Tom replied. "I figured you had enough on your mind without planning menus."

"Thanks, Tom. Matt and I went over to Mr. Rawlins's trailer. I told you about the money he had there. We thought we'd better bring it home and keep it safe."

"You never know what might have happened if you'd left

170

it there. He was working so hard to save for his grandkids down in Baltimore. Be a shame if anything happened to it. Did you get it okay?"

"Oh, yeah, we got it. Mr. Rawlins's son was there. He and Mom got to arguing so hard we forgot all about the money until he had left."

"You're kidding me!"

"I wish he was. You know me — 'Nancy Hansen, Crusader.' He really has a tremendous amount of bitterness toward his father. I wanted him to see there was some good in his father after all."

"Like Darth Vader," John said.

"What're you going to do with the money now, Nan?"

"I'll give it to him when he comes back. Mr. Rawlins is being buried in the military cemetery at Fort Indiantown Gap. I offered to arrange the funeral. I'm sure Bishop Adams won't mind."

"Maybe you'd better ask him first."

"Tom, am I out of line again?"

"No, Nan, you're not. You just throw your heart over the windmill. I happen to like it, but it might be a good idea to invite the bishop if we're having a funeral. Want me to call him?"

"Maybe you'd better."

18

O<small>N</small> T<small>HURSDAY</small>, M<small>ATT AND</small> C<small>INDI</small> <small>CHECKED OUT OF SCHOOL EARLY</small>. Cindi's mother took them to the chapel, on the ridge not far from the high school. There were only a few cars lined up next to the black Simpson Mortuary hearse.

"There's Hal Rawlins's car," Matt said, pointing to the green Pulsar with Maryland plates. "I wasn't sure he'd come."

"Why wouldn't he?" Cindi's mother asked.

"Mr. Rawlins was an alcoholic, Sister Thompson. His son hated his dad. We met him the other night, and he didn't have one good thing to say about his father."

"I won't sing 'O, My Father,' then," Cindi said. "He wouldn't understand."

They walked into the chapel. Bishop Adams already was seated on the stand, Matt's mother next to him. Cindi's mother sat down at the piano and began the prelude music. Cindi took a seat near her.

Matt looked at the handful of people in the pews. Hal Rawlins, his wife, and two daughters sat on the next-to-front row. Tom sat behind them with John. Sister Adams sat with Sister Jones, the Relief Society president. Behind them, Matt was surprised to see the long-haired service station attendant next to a man Matt didn't recognize. He looked around as someone came up the aisle behind him. It was Mrs. Satterfield.

"I didn't really know him," she whispered, "but I thought I should come. I did work with him."

She slid into the pew. Matt sat next to her.

"It was nice of you to come," he said.

"He must have been a lonely man," she replied.

Sister Thompson finished her piece, and Bishop Adams stood up. He looked over the small congregation drawn together by the accidental death of a recovering alcoholic. He wondered what comfort he could give them. In researching Harold Rawlins's life, he'd found much heartache and sorrow and very little joy. His eyes rested on Matt Hansen. "Sister Cindi Thompson will sing the opening hymn. Matthew Hansen will give the invocation."

Cindi stood near the piano. Strains of "I Know That My Redeemer Lives" filled the chapel. Matt wondered what he should pray for. He'd only attended three funerals, including his father's. He had no idea what to say. Cindi finished her song. As Matt walked up the aisle, he said a silent prayer. Afterwards, Matt couldn't remember exactly what he'd said. He remembered praying of love, of hope, and of understanding, but he knew the words had come from somewhere outside himself. They must have been all right, because the bishop smiled and murmured, "Well done," as Matt sat down next to his mother.

Bishop Adams searched the faces of the mourners as he adjusted the microphone. "Where is Harold Rawlins today?" he began.

"It would be easy for some of us to assume that he is with God. It would be equally easy for others to believe he was too far from the kingdom of God to assume any such thing." He looked at Hal Rawlins.

"I'm not attempting to excuse Harold Rawlins's weaknesses or deny the grief they brought to those he should have loved most dearly. As we search our own hearts, we realize that we are beset with faults that require charity on the part of our friends and families. We investigate our souls and find much that we should change. But we also find much good within ourselves, as I have in the life of Harold Rawlins.

"Harold Rawlins was a veteran of World War II, a retired Army master sergeant. That tells us what he did for a living. It also tells us much about his life. According to a letter from his mother that he kept until his death, Harold Rawlins ran away from home when he was only sixteen, following a particularly brutal beating from his father, who also was an alcoholic. In 1941, he joined the Army, fighting in the South Pacific. From his original battalion of five hundred men, only three returned home.

"Mr. Rawlins brought with him the Bronze Star, the Silver Star, and Purple Heart with Oakleaf Cluster, but he left his friends on the shores of those Pacific islands. They never left his memory. He thought about them; he talked about them; he asked why.

"In more than forty years, their suffering never left him. He had nothing in his experience to help him understand the carnage he had seen. In his despair, Harold Rawlins blamed God for the horrors he had seen, and he turned away from his source of strength and comfort.

"We don't have control over some of the adversities that come into our lives, but we do have control over how we choose to deal with them. If we choose wisely, adversity can become a blessing in our lives. We can become Christ-like.

"We can learn from our suffering just as our Savior did. But in order to do this, we must follow his example of humility, obedience, and love. If we are fortunate, or perhaps wise, we start early on the path toward the Savior. We no longer ask why sorrow comes in our lives; we ask what the Lord would have us learn from it.

"Though late in his life, Harold Rawlins found the beginning of that path and started to walk it. He was reaching outward, replacing his own self-concern with concern for others.

174

He was attempting to throw off the chains of a lifetime. Those of us who knew him were aware of his struggles and his efforts to make amends.

"Where is Harold Rawlins? The scriptures give answers to our questions. They tell us that our spirits go to a place of waiting and teaching, rather than to an immediate judgment. Today Harold Rawlins is being taught principles he only dimly understood here. He may be meeting friends who died on those beaches so many years ago, those he offended in this life, or those who offended him. I believe, as Matt prayed, that reconciliations may be taking place.

"Is Harold Rawlins a different person now than the man we knew? I don't think so. We must all overcome our sins before we enter the kingdom of God. He still has sins to overcome before he has met the requirements of the justice of God, but the Savior prepared the way for him to do this.

"The scriptures tell us plainly that Jesus was acquainted with suffering, with sorrow, with bitterness, with betrayal, and with anger. Through his wounds, we can be healed, not only of our sins, but of all the painful burdens of this life. Harold Rawlins had begun, though late in his life, to claim the mercy of our Savior. That mercy is available to all who will reach for it.

"As your brother, Harold Rawlins, good-bye. I'm sorry I never knew you." The bishop stood silently for a moment, then continued, "Cindi will sing 'Amazing Grace,' one of Mr. Rawlins's favorite songs. The closing prayer will be given by his employer, Nancy Hansen. Those who wish may accompany the body to Fort Indiantown Gap for burial with full military honors. When we return, a luncheon will be served for the family and friends." The bishop sat down.

When the service was over, Hal Rawlins and his family followed the casket through the side door of the chapel.

"Hang on a minute," Matt said to his mom. He caught up

with the service station attendant in the foyer. "Hey, thanks for coming."

"I figured I ought to. Like I told you, he used to talk about the war. I didn't pay much attention. He seemed like just another old drunk. Goes to show you, don't it? You can't ever tell about people."

"That's a fact," Matt agreed. "You want to ride out to the cemetery with us?"

"Thanks, man, but I got to work."

"See you around," Matt said as they walked through the double doors.

Tom, John, and Matt's mother were standing beside Tom's truck, talking with the man Matt hadn't recognized. Cindi and her mother joined the group as Matt walked up. Nancy spoke. "This is Mr. Simmons, Mr. Rawlins's landlord."

"Thanks for cleaning out the trailer, Mrs. Hansen," Mr. Simmons said. "It's not much, but I can usually find somebody to live there. Rawlins had been there quite a while. I could count on him. He was a good man in his own way. Nice funeral." He nodded to the group and walked to his car.

"Do you want to ride with us?" Cindi asked John.

"I'm going to ride with Tom," he replied.

"How about if we both ride with your mom?" Tom said.

They climbed into the Hansens' car. Sister Thompson and Cindi followed them from the parking lot. There were only five cars in the procession that wound its way down Skyline Drive to Highway 81. A forty-minute drive took them to the military cemetery at Fort Indiantown Gap.

A canopy had been erected above the open grave. As the hearse pulled up, the eight-man honor guard stood at attention. The sergeant in charge saluted the hearse.

The Rawlins family were escorted between the double row of soldiers. The sergeant slowly saluted the casket, which the eight soldiers carried. They lowered the casket onto the bier.

176

Sergeant Wilson took a folded flag and handed it to the first soldier. From man to man, the flag unfolded. The honor guard took a step back, drawing the flag taut over the casket.

Bishop Adams motioned to Cindi who stepped to the graveside. "Following Cindi's song," Bishop Adams said, "Tom Stratford will dedicate the grave."

The sun broke through the winter clouds as Cindi began to sing:

> Abide with me; 'tis eventide,
> And lone will be the night
> If I cannot commune with thee,
> Nor find in thee my light.
> The darkness of the world, I fear,
> Would in my home abide.
> O Savior, stay this night with me;
> Behold, 'tis eventide.
> O Savior, stay this night with me;
> Behold, 'tis eventide.

Cindi's voice died away. Tom stood and bowed his head, "Our Father in Heaven, we dedicate this grave as the resting place for the body of our brother Harold Rawlins and pray that it may rest lightly here, that his spirit may free itself of the chains that bound it here, that he may grow in spirit until he may be reunited with those he loved and come forth in the morning of the first resurrection."

At the conclusion of the prayer, Sergeant Wilson announced, "A twenty-one-gun salute will now be given." The firing-squad sergeant gave a command. Seven soldiers raised their rifles and fired. Twice more the guns fired in unison. An unseen bugler lifted his trumpet and played "Taps." As the mournful notes died away, the honor guard slowly folded the flag. Sergeant Wilson held it up for all to see and dropped three cartridges within its folds. He presented the flag to Hal Rawlins, who took it, head bowed. The sergeant saluted, turned, and marched the honor guard away.

Nancy was crying quietly, and Matt's eyes stung. He realized that he had been holding his breath. Hal Rawlins gripped the flag tightly as he walked to his car.

Tom and the Hansens were quiet on the way to the chapel. Finally Matt broke the silence. "It seems like such a waste. To be so brave and all that and still make such a mess of his life. I guess when you have to, you can fight. It's the day-to-day living that's tough."

"That's the truth!" Tom agreed. "Well, I hope Hal Rawlins feels a little better about his father now. It was a good funeral, Nan. I'm glad you pushed for it."

"People usually are glad—after it's all over. It's while I'm pushing that they don't like it."

"There're still a few people who feel threatened by a strong woman."

"What about you, Tom?"

"Me? Doesn't bother me a bit. Who'd want a partner you'd have to drag kicking and complaining into the celestial kingdom?"

Nancy watched Tom drive, a thoughtful look on her face.

"Mom, what are we gonna have for lunch?"

"I don't know, John. The Relief Society is fixing it."

"I hope there's lots. I'm hungry."

"Always!" said Matt.

The sisters were busy in the kitchen when Matt's family arrived. Two long tables had been set up in the Relief Society room next to the kitchen. The Rawlins family was already seated. Matt's mother sat across the table from Hal's wife. Tom sat down next to Nancy. He shook hands across the table with Hal.

The spicy smell of lasagna filled the room as Sister Jones removed two large pans from the oven. Bowls of salad and whole wheat rolls were already on the table. Sister Jones, Sister Adams, and Sister Thompson moved around the table, serving plates. When everyone was served, the women sat down next to the bishop. He squeezed his wife's shoulder. "Since you ladies prepared the food, why don't one of you bless it for us?"

Sister Jones did. For a few moments, there was only silence around the table as salad, dressing, rolls, and butter were passed. Finally, Hal Rawlins looked up. "I don't rightly know what I expected when Mrs. Hansen offered to arrange my father's funeral, but it certainly wasn't anything like this. You've treated us as though we belonged here. Thank you."

"I didn't know your father when he was alive," Bishop Adams said, "but I feel as though I do now. Not only as I heard about him, but as I looked over the few papers he left, I began to get a picture of him. In spite of his problems, he tried to do his duty. He failed with you, but he never forgot that, either."

"He talked about your kids a lot," Matt said.

"That's true," Nancy added. "And he was a good employee, even when he was sick. At first, he was terribly ill at ease with the kids, but he stuck with it, and he got better. Didn't he, Cindi?"

"He sure did. He always brought candy canes to give the kids."

"I didn't know he'd been sick, but then I wouldn't have. I haven't talked to him in three or four years."

"He was dying," Tom said. "Cancer. He'd just gotten the tests back a couple of days before he was killed."

"He told me he didn't think he had much time left," Nancy said. "He knew what a mess he'd made of his life, and he wanted to make amends. He knew how you felt, and he didn't blame you. He had just one goal, and that was to leave something for your girls."

She smiled at the two girls and removed the large manila

179

envelope from her purse. "This is his legacy to you girls," she said, "but your mother'd better take care of it." She handed the envelope to Mrs. Rawlins.

Hal's wife dumped the contents on the table. A Bronze Star, a Silver Star, the Purple Heart, and the rubber-band wrapped pile of bills fell out.

"What in the world?" she said.

"There's $1,720 there, Mrs. Rawlins. Mr. Rawlins must have been saving for a long time. He only made $4.75 an hour working for me part-time. He wanted his grandchildren to have it."

Hal Rawlins fingered the military decorations. He stared at the stack of bills. Tears came to his eyes. "That's a lot of bottles he didn't buy."

"I don't think he bought one while he worked for me," Nancy said.

"We talked a few times," Tom said. "He didn't take any credit for your success, but he was proud that you'd overcome things he hadn't been able to. From what he said, alcoholism goes back a long way on both sides of your family."

"I know it does. I decided clear back when I was an MP in the service to leave it alone."

His wife spoke, "When we went to a class for adult children of alcoholics, they explained how the whole family is hurt when one member is an alcoholic."

Hal Rawlins nodded. "Maybe we can put it behind us now. I'm interested in what the bishop and Mr. Stratford said about my father having time to change. I always figured that, when you were dead, that was it."

"We believe the spirit can progress and change until the final judgment," Bishop Adams said, "which the Bible tells us isn't until the end of the world. That's why Jesus went and preached to the souls of the dead."

"He did what?" Mrs. Rawlins asked.

"First Peter 4:6. Between the time of his death and resurrection, the Savior visited the spirits of those who were dead and taught them the gospel so that they could live according to his teachings. We believe that there's great hope for your father, and for you all to be united again."

"That'd be interesting, if it were true," Hal said.

"Oh, it's true," Nancy said. "I can tell you from my own experience that people who've loved us don't forget us just because they're dead. And they can change."

"Hmmm," Hal said, picking up his fork.

19

CINDY, MATT, AND BEEF WERE ALREADY SEATED when Chico came into the cafeteria on Friday. Laura Satterfield was just ahead of him in line. Matt saw Laura turn around and say something to him. Chico smiled and motioned toward their table. After getting her food, she followed him across the room and sat down next to Beef. "Laura is on the math team with Matt and me," Chico said. "I told you about her."

Beef looked stunned, "Chico didn't say you were beautiful."

Laura looked pleased.

"She is also very smart. Dr. Samuels says we'll win the district competition. I am not so sure. It would be wonderful."

"It would sure help you get your scholarship," Cindi said.

"Oh, yes, but I think of my father also."

Laura spoke, "Matt said your father is a famous mathematician."

"He was," Chico said. "He's dead now."

"It must be hard to lose your dad," Cindi said. "I don't know what I'd do without mine."

"Mine's gone so much that we hardly ever see him," Laura said. "He never talks to us when he's home. Mom says it's because he can't tell us about so many things. His work's dangerous, and he doesn't want us to worry, so we never know what's happening until it's over and we read about it in the papers."

"What does your dad do?" Cindi asked.

Matt watched Chico for his reaction.

"He's a Treasury agent."

"Investigating income taxes and stuff?" Beef asked.

"My dad's a drug agent. He's head of the regional task force."

Chico blinked. "Are you flying tonight with Tom?" he asked Matt.

"Nope, darn it. I'm playing Santa Claus. Beef's cutting out on me."

"How can you do that to us?" Cindi teased.

"It's not hard. Over Christmas, we always go to my grandparents in Pittsburgh for our family reunion. Both my uncles are school teachers, so it works out real well."

"I'd think summer would be even better," Laura said.

"Car sales are down between Christmas and New Year's. They're up in the summer. We don't travel in the summer."

"They own Kowalski Motors," Matt explained.

"You mean Kowalski Motors owns us," Beef corrected.

"Sounds like my dad," Laura said. "He's a workaholic too. What about yours, Cindi?"

"He puts in a lot of hours, but I don't think he's a workaholic. He says his job supports his career."

"If his job isn't his career," Beef asked, "what is?"

"He and Mom say having a family is their career. Dad's shop and Mom's daycare just support the family."

"That's sure different," Laura said.

"So Tom is flying alone," Chico asked. "Will he go to Buffalo?"

"He most always does. Say, Chico . . . " He looked at Laura. "Yes?"

"Oh, never mind. I was just thinking."

"Watch it, man! That's dangerous," Beef said.

"Especially when you're not used to it," agreed Laura.

"I hope your calculator quits working in the middle of an exam."

183

"No problem. I'll do Trachtenberg," she said.

"What's Trachtenberg?"

"A speed system of mathematics," Chico said. "My father knew the man who developed it. He invented it while he was in a Nazi concentration camp. Instead of working everything out on paper, you just —"

Beef interrupted, "Could we talk about something else? I'm eating."

"I agree," Cindi said. "My sister Shauna's got all the math talent for our whole family."

While Matt played Santa that night, he thought of Tom. In his mind, he went over the external checks with Tom. He was with him when Tom taxied the plane over to pick up his load. He saw the courier and wondered whether there'd be a shipment of boxes in the nose from "Cruise, International." But when it came time for Tom to lift the 310 off the ground, Matt wasn't there. He was solidly on the ground, the toddler on his lap telling him what she wanted for Christmas.

Cindi came back to talk with Matt during a break between customers. Matt asked, "Do you think Beef'll join the Church?"

"I don't know. He likes it when he's with us, but that's not having a testimony. His dad won't want him to get baptized."

"But he fights with his dad all the time. You think he'll do what his father wants?"

"I've seen people who can't break loose from their parents even though their relationships are terrible. I don't think he'll go against his dad, especially if he starts going with Laura."

"I thought he liked you."

"Wake up and smell the Postum, Matt! I was a challenge to him. It was a part of his rivalry with you. He's not as interested in me anymore. Laura's a lot more his type. You saw them today."

"He seemed pretty interested when he talked to me about it. I told him we were just friends."

184

Cindi was quiet a moment. "Maybe if we'd been better friends I could have helped you more when you got hurt."

"Nobody could have helped me then, Cindi. I was still too mad. I just wanted to be left alone. When I knew I'd never play football again, I didn't know who I was anymore. Ever since my dad died, football was all I'd thought about. I didn't know how to relate to people any other way."

"And you know now?"

Something in her tone made Matt look closely at her. "Maybe I'm learning. When you get involved with other people, you find out how small your own troubles are. It gives you perspective, like flying. Your own corner of the world seems real big until you're looking at it from up there. Then you see how small it really is, and how much else there is out there."

More customers came, and Cindi went back to her camera. They were busy until the mall closed.

"Give you a ride home, Cindi?"

"Thanks. I hate to have Dad come all the way over here."

They walked into the still-crowded parking lot. Headlights flashed on all over the lot. Long lines of cars were backed up at the mall exits. "I'm glad it's the last weekend before Christmas," Cindi said. "It's been fun, but I've sure spent a lot of hours on my feet."

"Are you working next week?"

"Dad said I could work Tuesday night and all day Christmas Eve, if your mother needs me. He feels bad that he and Mom can't do more about school for me."

"Where do you think you'll go?"

"If I can get a scholarship, I'll go to BYU like Shauna did. If not, I'll have to go to the community college. What about you?"

"When I was playing football, I was going to apply for scholarships to the good football schools. I haven't decided where to go now. I don't want to go to Penn State."

"Why don't you apply to the Y? It'd be good preparation for your mission."

"My mission?"

"You know, that two-year thing, dark suits, name tags."

"Oh, yeah! Where you lose your girlfriend and your hair."

"That's it! Since you don't have a girlfriend, all you have to worry about is your hair."

Matt was quiet as he drove down Simpson Ferry Road to St. John's Church Road and turned right.

"Matt, aren't you going on a mission?"

"I always figured I would. It was, like, another ticket to punch. Now, I'm not sure. How can I teach people they've got a Heavenly Father who loves them when I'm not sure of it myself?"

Cindi put her hand on Matt's arm. "I know Heavenly Father loves us."

"I don't have any trouble believing he loves you," Matt replied. "Everybody loves you. It's me I'm not sure about. I've never been sure he loved me. I don't even know if my own father loved me."

"I wish I could give you that."

"I guess nobody can. I'll have to find it out myself. Either it comes or it doesn't."

"It doesn't just come, Matt. You have to work at it. Have you prayed about it?" The car swung around a corner.

"Not lately." Matt braked in front of Cindi's house. They both got out, and he walked her to the door. He was silent.

"Think about going to the Y," Cindi said.

"I will. See you at the ward dinner."

"You might," Cindi said. "The Laurels offered to help take care of the nursery." She pushed the door open and slipped inside.

Saturday afternoon, Matt helped his mother pack table decorations. Different families had signed up to decorate tables, and each one brought its own tablecloth, dishes, and decorations. "Run up to the attic, Matt, and bring the little artificial tree down. We'll use it for a centerpiece."

When they got to the chapel, the elders quorum was still setting up tables and chairs. Matt went to help them while John carried boxes into the cultural hall. Two tables had been pulled together for each host family to decorate. Nancy spread a red plastic tablecloth over hers and covered the plastic with white lace cloths. She set the tree where the two tables came together. While John carefully unwrapped cornhusk dolls and red bows, she arranged artificial greenery and candles down the table.

"Mom, can I decorate the tree, please?"

"Let's have Matt do it. You can help put the knives and forks around."

"I'd rather put the ornaments on."

Matt had finished putting up tables and chairs. He returned to their table in time to hear the discussion. If John decorated the tree, he could imagine what it would look like. "Hey, kid, I need a turn to help."

Nancy flashed him a grateful smile.

"Let's hurry. I've got to go pick up Chico."

When Matt and Chico returned, the cultural hall was full. The food had been set up buffet-style, and lines were forming. Matt saw Jeanette Jones sitting at the end of their table. He saw Tom next to his mother in the line, but he didn't see Dr. Samuels anywhere.

By the time Matt and Chico had filled their plates, the Jones family and Tom and Matt's mother were already seated. Matt motioned Chico to a seat next to Jennifer Jones and introduced them.

"Glad you could make it," Tom said across the table to Chico.

"Thanks for your help," Chico said.

What help? thought Matt. "I guess Dr. Samuels isn't coming."

"He called me," Tom said. "His little boy is back in the hospital."

"That's too bad," Nancy said. "What's the matter?"

"Respiratory problems. I guess he's had a couple of bouts every winter since he was a baby."

"That's really hard," Sister Jones said. "I remember how much time we spent at the hospital with Jeanette the first few years."

"Mom and Dad just about lived there," Jennifer said. "But it was worth it," she added, leaning over and giving Jeanette a hug.

"Do the Samuelses have other children?" Nancy asked.

"I don't think so," Tom said.

"I didn't even know he was married," Matt said. "Nobody at school knows anything about him."

"I suspect he wants it that way," Tom said.

"How'd you get to know him, Tom?"

"I met him at the airport. We're both pilots. We went to the same school, majored in the same thing. We have a lot of common ground. He's from over by Trenton—not too far from my folks' home in Mt. Holly."

"I didn't know your folks lived in Mt. Holly," Nancy said. "Isn't that where the John Woolman home is?"

"The one he built for his daughter? It's open for tours."

"I'd love to see it."

"Who's John Woolman?" Matt asked.

"He was a Quaker missionary during the 1700s," said Brother Jones. "He went all up and down the east coast, preaching against slavery."

Matt remembered that Jennifer had said her ancestors were Quakers.

"That's not all he preached about," Nancy said. "I read

some of his journal and several essays at the Y. He sounds like the brethren. His essay 'On Merchandising' really affected me. I decided if I ever had a business, I'd run it like he said a Christian should."

"He was quite a man," Tom said.

"Did you ever read his letter to his wife?" Sister Jones asked.

"Just some excerpts."

"You'd like it. It reminds me of when Brigham Young and Heber C. Kimball left Nauvoo for their mission to England."

Tom said, "Chico and Matt will probably read him in college. Where are you planning to go to school, Chico?"

"I'd like to go to Princeton, but I need a scholarship."

"Talk to Dr. Samuels," Tom suggested. "There's more aid available for Princeton than you'd think."

Conversation became general as they finished the meal. A member of the high priest group wheeled around a cart of desserts. When dessert was over, the Young Men wheeled garbage carts around for families who'd brought paper plates. Those who'd brought their own dishes scraped the plates into the carts and carefully stacked them in boxes to take home and wash.

"Hey, Tom," John asked, "are you gonna come home and help us wash dishes?"

"Oh, I might," said Tom, grinning at Nancy, "but I'm going over to the hospital first. I'd like to see how the Samuels are doing."

"Could we go along?" Matt asked.

"Let's wait until we've got the tables cleared away."

As the men folded tables and set up chairs in front of the stage for the program, Matt saw Cindi in the doorway. He walked over to her. "Dr. Samuels's little boy is in the hospital. Chico and I are going over with Tom after the cleanup's done."

"Do you think I could go too? I've never had a class from

189

him, but he was Shauna's favorite teacher in high school. He helped her get her scholarship."

"Are you ready to go?" Tom said as Matt and Cindi walked up.

"Sure," Matt said. "Is it okay if Cindi comes?"

Tom looked from Matt to Cindi. "Why not?"

Nancy turned from the boxes she and Sister Jones were packing. "Why don't you take this little tree along? Since it's artificial, they should let him have it in his room. Take my car, Tom. I can drive your truck home."

"Sounds good."

Chico carefully carried the decorated tree out to the Hansens' car. He held it up on his lap. Matt and Cindi sat in the back seat. A quarter hour later, they reached the hospital. Tom stopped at the desk and asked the nursing sister for the room number. They rounded the corner, entered the elevator, and rode to the third-floor pediatric ward.

"Hi, Cindi," the nurse at the desk said. "Are you still candy-striping?"

Cindi shook her head. "I've been working part-time at the mall."

"We could use you up here."

"I'll get back to it soon. Is it okay if we go down to 390?"

"Michael Samuels? As long as you don't stay too long. His parents are both there."

Tom tapped on the door. Dr. Samuels opened it. His wife, a pretty blond in her late thirties, sat in the corner chair, a counted-cross stitch frame in her lap. Her hands gripped the chair arms.

"Why, Tom, I didn't expect you." He looked beyond Tom to see Chico with the tree and Matt and Cindi behind him. Shock crossed his face, to be quickly replaced with his usual impassivity. "What have we here, a delegation?"

"We brought your little boy a Christmas tree," Cindi said

as she stepped forward and took the tree from Chico. Cindi set the tree on the chest across from the bed. Chico stepped over to the bedside of the blond child. The boy's eyes were closed. An I.V. was hooked up to one arm, which had been strapped to the bed to hold it still. His fingers were short, and Matt noticed that his ears seemed smaller than normal. A tube ran up his snub nose.

Chico bowed his head and crossed himself. *"El innocente de diós,"* he said softly.

"What did you say?" Mrs. Samuels said.

Chico looked at her. Matt saw tears in his eyes. "One of God's innocents," he explained. "My cousin is one. You are to be congratulated. Not everyone can be so trusted."

"Congratulated?" Dr. Samuels said incredulously. "I must confess I never expected that reaction from one of my students."

"I told you," Mrs. Samuels said, "that people are kind."

"You are less familiar with students than I, Marsha, if you think so."

Obviously, Chico and Cindi knew what was happening, and Tom didn't appear to be puzzled, but Matt was totally in the dark.

Mrs. Samuels must have seen his questioning look. "Michael has Down's syndrome," she said.

"You mean he's retarded?" Matt asked. No wonder Dr. Samuels seemed so unhappy.

"That's the least of it. He's had three open-heart surgeries. He also has serious respiratory problems."

"But, why?" asked Matt. He could have bitten his tongue as soon as the words were out of his mouth.

"It's my fault," Mrs. Samuels said. "I was so determined to get my advanced degrees. Of course, once I had my doctorate, I didn't want to waste my education. But after a few years, we

191

decided it was time to have a baby if we were going to. I wish we never had!"

"Marsha, it's not your fault," Dr. Samuels said in a tone of one who has repeated the same thing many times without believing or being believed.

Cindi knelt by Mrs. Samuels's chair. "I don't know a whole lot about Down's," she said, "but one thing I do know. It didn't happen because of your age. Dr. Samuels, do you remember my sister Shauna?"

"Of course. She was my top student, oh, five or six years ago when I first came to Cumberland Ridge."

"You remember that she went away to college. At the end of her sophomore year, she got married. Her first baby has Down's. Mrs. Samuels, she was twenty-two."

"My aunt, she also was young when Maria was born," Chico said.

"Shauna and Curt wanted to know why their baby has Down's. I think she read everything there was to read. She told me that eighty percent of Down's babies are born to women under thirty-five. They're looking at lots of things that might cause Down's, but the only thing Shauna found out for sure is that there's an extra chromosome in Down's kids. No one really knows why."

"Eighty percent!" Dr. Samuels said with astonishment. "Are you sure?"

"Shauna said so."

"How's your sister's baby?" his wife asked.

"Really well. They're involved in some alternative treatments with her. She's walking, and she's potty trained. She doesn't talk a whole lot, but she does talk. Of course, Shauna's really busy with Megan and a new baby."

"She has another baby?"

"It took a lot of nerve to try again, but they're glad they did."

192

Michael stirred. His eyes opened, wandered, then focused on his mother. Mrs. Samuels hurried to his side, reaching for his unstrapped hand.

"We'd better go," Tom said.

Dr. Samuels followed the little group from the room. Tom squeezed his shoulder. "You don't need to worry about these kids."

"I should have known," the math teacher replied. He sighed and straightened his shoulders.

"I'll call you in a day or two to see how it's going," Tom said.

"Thanks so much," Dr. Samuels said quietly.

No one felt like talking as Tom dropped Cindi and Chico off. When the two arrived at Matt's, the house was still dark. Tom pulled the car into the garage. As they walked up the sidewalk, Nancy drove in with Tom's pickup. Matt and Tom lifted the boxes from the back and carried them to the kitchen table.

"I'll wash, Matt can rinse, and you dry, Nancy. You know where things go."

"What can I do?" John asked.

"How about you carry the plates over to me," Tom said, "one at a time. Can you be careful with your mother's good dishes?"

"Of course," John said, and he was.

Nancy found a fresh towel. "How's Dr. Samuels's son?"

"He's got Down's syndrome, Nan. He's had three heart surgeries. Stewart says he has a lot of lung problems too."

"Mom, did you know Shauna Thompson had a baby with Down's?"

"Why, yes. Didn't you?"

"I don't remember hearing about it."

"I guess people don't talk about it much anymore. She must be nearly four. It was really hard on them at first, especially

193

Shauna's husband. You hear so much about Down's kids being born to women my age that it's a shock when somebody as young as Shauna has one."

"If you thought about all the things that could go wrong in this life," Tom said, "you'd sit in a corner and refuse to move."

"Not me," John said.

When the dishes were finished, they sat in the family room. Nancy plugged in the Christmas tree lights and turned off the chandelier. "We'd like you to have Christmas dinner with us, Tom."

"I'd sure like that, Nancy, but I'm leaving for Mt. Holly as soon as we shut down the Santa booth Christmas Eve. Since my brothers and sister are so far away, I always try to spend Christmas with my folks."

"Oh," Nancy replied.

"I'll be back Friday morning, Matt. We'll be flying as usual. Van Ryck gives only two nights off all year — Christmas Eve and Christmas."

20

It was a quiet Christmas that year. Matt and Tom crated the Santa booth Christmas Eve so that it could be shipped back the day after Christmas. Tom left for Mt. Holly; and Matt, John, and their mother had their usual Christmas Eve family home evening.

John was out of bed before daylight, but his mother refused to let him open his presents until they'd had breakfast and she'd put the turkey in the oven.

John was excited with his presents, especially the radio-controlled car Matt had gotten him. Nancy gave Matt a sheep-skin-lined coat like Tom's. The dress Cindi had helped them choose pleased her. Nancy served Christmas dinner at two. The table seemed empty somehow without Tom. Matt made it a point to tell his mother how good everything was, but Christmas seemed curiously flat. Matt kept expecting something to happen, but nothing did. He finally fell asleep on the couch, reading *The Alliance,* a Gerald Lund novel the bishop had given him.

About four o'clock the doorbell rang. Matt's mother jumped up to answer it. Parked in front of the house was a grey van with "Carlisle Floral" on the side. A smile lit up Nancy's face as she accepted an arrangement of Christmas-red roses. As she opened the card, the smile faded, and a flicker of surprise crossed her face. "I didn't expect this," she said, handing the card to Matt.

"For the love you've shown us, thank you, and Merry Christ-

195

mas," Matt read. "We found one of your churches near our house. Hal and Eileen Rawlins."

Matt and John were in the kitchen eating turkey sandwiches about six-thirty when lights swung into the driveway. Matt looked out the door. "Hey, Mom," he called, "Tom's here."

Nancy came into the kitchen as John opened the door for Tom. He was carrying two small packages. "I didn't expect you back till tomorrow," she said.

"Seemed as if I'd done everything I needed to do, so I came home."

"Well, take your coat off and stay a while."

"You want a sandwich?" Matt asked.

"They're good," John said. "I've got cranberry sauce on mine."

"I think I might."

"I'll make it, Mom." Matt got up and began slicing turkey.

When they'd finished eating, Tom picked up the packages from the chair beside him. "Here, John, this is for you."

"Wow!" John said as he tore off the paper, "now I can take my scriptures to church just like the big kids."

"It's got your name on it," Tom said. "Won't be long until you can read it yourself."

Nancy smiled at Tom. "Thanks," she said. "I wouldn't have thought of giving him a copy of the Book of Mormon. Matt didn't get his until he was eight."

"I started reading it when I was in first grade," Tom said. "I wouldn't be surprised if John does too."

"You bet!" John said.

"I'll help you," Matt added.

"Wonders never cease," Nancy said *sotto voce*.

Tom handed Matt an envelope. Inside was a hand-lettered certificate that read, "Good for two hours' flying time." "I've arranged to rent a Cessna 152 so you can do some daytime flying," Tom said.

196

"Thanks, Tom! This is great! When can we go?"

"Sometime next week when the weather's good. We'll practice some stalls."

"Stalls? On purpose?"

"Sure. If you have a stall in the air, you've got to know how to recover quickly. New pilots try to lift the nose to gain altitude when they stall. That's the worst thing you can do. We'll have you practice until it's second nature for you to drop the nose and open the throttles."

"Matt, are you gonna be a pilot too?" John asked.

"Probably," his mother said. "He just as well be like the rest of the men around here."

Tom was quiet for a moment. Then he picked up the other package. He hefted it. Finally he said, "I hope you like this, Nan."

Nancy laid the package on the table, removed the ribbon, and split the Scotch tape carefully along the seam. Reverently, she picked up the worn leather book and opened the cover. She showed Matt the title page. "The Works of John Woolman in Two Parts," it read. "Philadelphia: Printed by Joseph Cruikshank, in Market Street, between Second and Third Streets, M,DCC,LXXIV."

"That's 1774," she said. "A first edition! Wherever did you find it?"

"Oh, I've got a friend who deals in antique books over in East Brunswick. He found it for me Tuesday in New York. My folks and I drove over and picked it up today. We always have our dinner on Christmas Eve anyway."

"It's wonderful! Listen to this, Matt." She turned carefully to the back and began to read from "On Merchandising":

"Where the treasures of pure love are opened and we obediently follow him who is the light of life, the mind becomes chaste; and a care is felt, that the unction from the holy one may be our leader in every undertaking."

"That means we listen to the Holy Ghost," Nancy explained to John. She resumed reading:

"In being crucified to the world, broken off from that friendship which is enmity with God, and dead to the customs and fashions which have not their foundation in the truth; the way is prepared to lowliness in outward living, and to a disentanglement from those snares which attend the love of money; and where the faithful friends of Christ are so situated that merchandise appears to be their duty, they feel a restraint from proceeding farther than he owns their proceeding; being convinced that 'we are not our own but are bought with a price, that none of us may live to ourselves, but to him who died for us.' 2 Corin. v. 15. Thus they are taught not only to keep to a moderate advance and uprightness in their dealings; but to consider the tendency of their proceeding; to do nothing which they know would operate against the cause of universal righteousness; and to keep continually in view the spreading of the peaceable kingdom of Christ among mankind."

Nancy looked up from the book. "I read it in college, and it's always stuck with me. We have a duty to build the kingdom even in our business dealings. I don't care if I never get rich."

"Neither do I," Tom said, "as you can tell from my job." He grinned at Matt.

"But you've got to have money," Matt objected.

"Of course," Tom replied. "The house John Woolman built in Mt. Holly isn't a slum. What he's saying is that you shouldn't fill up your life with more things than you actually need for your family. Instead, you should build what he called the peaceable kingdom of Christ."

"He became so successful," Nancy said, "that he cut back on his business to have time for his spiritual life."

"He makes a good case for the Word of Wisdom too," Tom said.

"The sad thing is that he was misunderstood by so many of his own Quaker friends and neighbors."

"You notice how often that happens when somebody's trying to live the gospel now?" Tom asked.

"Oh, yes!"

"I thought you might have." Tom chuckled.

Nancy nodded. "I don't know how to thank you enough, Tom. I don't think I've ever had a finer present."

"If you're pleased, that's all the thanks I want."

"I want another piece of pumpkin pie," John said.

"Sounds good," Tom agreed.

21

TOM AND MATT LOADED THE 310 FRIDAY NIGHT. The shipment for Cruise, International, in Buffalo was larger than the first one Matt had seen, but it was still small enough to fit in the nose.

Matt was surprised at how natural taking off had become. The gauges were still formidable, but he was beginning to understand the radios. He handled both the radios and the aircraft until time to descend at Philly International. Matt needed only minimum coaching as he began landing procedures. The weather in Philadelphia was cloudy, so they made an instrument landing. Although Tom covered him on the controls, Tom let Matt touch the plane down and taxi to the cargo area. "Not bad," he said as Matt switched off the engines.

"I can hardly wait until next week."

"I'm looking forward to it myself. I started you out backwards. You've done all your tough flying first."

After they unloaded the checks, Tom and Matt transferred the boxes from the nose into the cargo space behind the seats. Matt taxied toward the runway and waited for tower clearance, then the plane sped down the runway and lifted off into the air, Matt setting their course northwest for Buffalo.

It was overcast and cold with flurries of snow. "I'll be glad when winter's over," Tom said. "Did you have a good Christmas?"

"This is the first year I've earned all the money for the gifts I bought. That made a difference."

"A little sacrifice adds to the gift, doesn't it?"

"You must have worked hard to find that book. Mom really liked it."

"A woman needs more than hearts and flowers sometimes."

"She got flowers too. The Rawlins family sent her a big bunch of red roses Christmas afternoon. She was surprised when she saw who they were from. She should have known you wouldn't send her flowers."

"I might sometime. I didn't say she didn't need flowers. I said she needed more than flowers. Sort of a hyacinth for her soul."

The plane rocked and bucked through the clouds. Matt was more and more grateful for the radios. Tom keyed the mike for permission to land in Buffalo. Matt looked at the boxes behind them. "Tom, what if this stuff really is drugs?"

"Not our business, Matt. That's the drug boys' job."

"How're they going to know?"

"They've got ways."

Tom began his approach. "You want to take it in?"

Matt shook his head. Tom had had two weeks to think about the boxes. Matt didn't understand his attitude, but when he thought about it, Tom had spent the last fifteen years trying hard not to be involved. Maybe he just didn't want to get drawn into the problem. Matt didn't feel comfortable with that. He might never be the crusader that his mother was, but he believed in doing what was right. If the Cruz brothers were shipping drugs in Tom's plane, they ought to be stopped.

Tom taxied the Cessna around the building. Morrison's twin engine blue Aztec waited on the ramp. Tom swung the 310 between the Aztec and the building. As Tom cut the engines and inserted the gust lock, Matt saw the Aztec's door swing open.

"Tom, watch out!" Matt said, suddenly wary.

Tom didn't seem to hear him as he climbed out onto the wing and met Morrison on the ground beside the Cessna.

201

"You're late, Stratford. What took you chaps so long? Your service said you left Harrisburg at nine."

"I went to Philly first," Tom said calmly. "What's the rush?"

Matt had joined them on the ground. Morrison held out a manifest. "Here's my authorization to pick up the shipment for Cruise, International."

"Do you know what's in it?" Matt asked.

Morrison glared at him. "How should I know — I'm just the pilot."

"Are you taking it directly from us?" Tom asked.

"I'm authorized to accept their shipments. Now, if you two Yanks will help me load the stuff into my plane, we can all get out of here."

"Get the cargo door, Matt."

Matt opened the cargo compartment and swung the door back against the fuselage. He pulled out a box and handed it to Tom, who carried it around the tail to Morrison. Morrison loaded the box into the Aztec.

They'd transferred half a dozen boxes when Morrison paused and pounded his gloved hands together. "I've had about all I can stand of northern winters," he said. "I'm sure tired of living in cold country."

"Maybe you ought to move to the Bahamas," Tom said.

"I'm going to. I've had all the snow and ice I ever want."

Matt carried the last box around the tail of the plane. Tom stepped quickly to meet him, took the box from his arms, and carried it to Morrison. As he reached the Aztec's cargo door, Tom's foot trod on a patch of icy snow, and he fell. The box landed under him.

Matt stared, appalled, at the plastic protruding from the broken corner of the box. He quickly reached Tom and bent down to help him up. Morrison stuck his arm into the cargo door and brought out a .38 caliber service revolver. "Into the building, quickly!" he said.

While he slowly brushed snow from his clothes, Tom watched the Canadian.

"Hurry up!" Morrison demanded, motioning with the gun. His hand didn't look steady to Matt, but the gun looked enormous pointed at them.

"I hope they're paying you a bundle," Tom said. "I wouldn't have sold our friendship for twice the cargo you just loaded."

"You first, kid. Move!"

Matt took one step, another, then a third toward the darkened cargo building. He stopped near the door.

"Go on!" Morrison screamed.

"Go in the building, Matt," Tom said, still calm.

Matt pushed the door open. He turned to look at Morrison. "Get inside that building!" Morrison ordered.

Matt stood frozen. "Do it, Matt," Tom commanded. Matt walked into the cargo bay. Looking out the doorway, he saw Tom face Morrison. Tom stretched his arms, blocking the door. "This is as far as I go," Matt heard. "If you want to shoot me, you'll have to do it in the open. I haven't been a pilot all these years to die cooped up in a warehouse."

"Quit grandstanding! All I want to do is lock you and the kid in there long enough to haul my load out of here."

Matt didn't know what to do. He looked frantically around the cargo bay and saw some two by fours next to a stack of boxes. He picked one up as quietly as possible. Outside, he could hear Tom saying, "I don't believe that, and neither do you. You can't fly fast enough to get away. It's your last haul, Morrison."

"This is your only chance, Stratford."

"I'm not moving." Matt crept back to the door and peeked through the crack in the doorjamb. Tom continued, "You'll have to shoot, and it won't do you a bit of good. Matt's had long enough to get out the other door and get help."

Matt saw the .38 lift. Morrison's hand shook as he brought

the weapon forward. Matt couldn't leave Tom out there alone, but he was afraid the slightest move would set Morrison off. He was ready to charge through the door when Morrison's finger tightened on the trigger, and the hammer eared back. "There're worse things than dying," Tom said calmly.

Morrison swore—and lowered the gun. He spun around and made for the Aztec in a stumbling run.

Matt came out the door, the length of two by four in his hand. Tom gripped Matt's shoulder as they watched the pilot climb into the Aztec. The engines turned over and caught. The plane roared down the ramp toward its intersection with Taxiway Bravo. Before the Aztec reached the end of the building, a hook-and-ladder truck, lights flashing, pulled down the taxiway between the building and the ramp, blocking Morrison's escape. A uniformed figure with an Uzi climbed from the Dumpster near the end of the ramp, and a second man clambered over the chain-link fence.

The Aztec hesitated, swerved to the right, and began circling on its axis. Round and round and round it went, one engine racing as the other died. A man dropped off the fire truck and ran for the trailing edge of the wing. He leaped on and, after a struggle, wrenched open the door and reached inside. The second engine died, and the whirling Aztec coasted to a stop. From the doorway behind them, Tom and Matt heard a voice, "Sergeant Gauge, New York State Police. Come with me, please; we've got some talking to do."

"You bet we do!" Tom said.

Matt had never heard him so coldly furious. They followed the sergeant into the office where Matt had first met Morrison. They were joined by a plainclothesman and a typist prepared to take down their statements.

"You guys could have got us killed!" Tom said.

"It was a near thing," the plainclothesman agreed. "We had

a man in the building here, one on the roof, and a marksman just over the fence."

"Why didn't one of them do something?"

"Nothing we had on Morrison led us to think he was violent."

"You mean the cops knew about Morrison?" Matt asked.

"When Mr. Stratford contacted Mr. Satterfield's office in Harrisburg, we did a background check. Morrison did time some years ago for transporting, but there was a question about his guilt. He claimed he was unaware of the shipments. His copilot might have been the one who was involved, but the Florida police didn't have any evidence against him, so Morrison went to jail. After he got out, he flew for a freight company that might have been part of the international chain, but we had no hard evidence against him. That's what we hoped to get tonight."

"I hope you've got enough!" Tom said.

"We got plenty. Our man on the roof took photos of Morrison with the stuff in his hands actually loading it into his plane. We got him on tape when he told you he was authorized to accept the shipment. This time he couldn't have denied that he handled the stuff. Our only real mistake was not having a man closer in case Morrison became violent. I can only say, Mr. Stratford, that I'm sorry. He wasn't known to ever carry a gun, but that's no excuse in my business."

Tom rubbed his forehead. "Well, I can tell you, I was scared to death. I expected you guys to have someone here, but there wasn't a sign. I figured I'd better keep Matt in the dark so he wouldn't let anything slip."

"Yeah!" Matt said in disgust. "And then I just about blew the lid off. I had to ask him what was in the shipment."

"You'd been wondering for a long time, Matt," Tom said. "It takes practice for an honest person to learn not to say what's

205

on his mind. Sometimes I think it's a shame we ever have to learn."

"When you're dealing with criminals, you have to learn fast," Detective Gauge said. "Otherwise, you're dead. I don't suggest you go into police work, young man."

"I'm not about to," Matt agreed.

"We were in good order," the plainclothesman continued, "until Morrison started you two toward the building. Our man with the rifle had a clear field of fire until you walked past the tail of your plane. By the time he had worked his way into a position he could shoot from, one of you was in his line of fire. Once Matt was inside the building, we were better off. We'd have tried for a shot just as you stepped inside the door. Whatever possessed you to defy him?"

"I was responsible for Matt. When I got into this, I knew it was dangerous. I'd made a choice. Matt hadn't. I was counting on our friendship, mine and Morrison's, but when a guy pulls a gun on you, he's already told you what he's willing to do. You've got no call to trust him after that. I figured he just wanted us where it was a little more private. He was already coming apart at the seams. He'd have killed us for sure once he got us inside the building."

"He was primed to shoot, all right," the plainsclothesman agreed. "When he couldn't get away, he shot himself. He's dead."

"Dead?" Tom said.

"When Damson finally got into the plane," Sergeant Gauge replied, "Morrison had his foot jammed against the rudder pedals, and a bullet through his brain."

Tom looked stunned. "We were friends for years, and I never knew him. If only—"

"If only you'd walked into the building with him," the sergeant said, "it would have been you and not him. I've been in this business long enough to know one thing: never cry over a drug runner!"

"I think we have all we need, Sergeant," the plainsclothesman said. "Notify ground control that they're cleared to leave."

The sergeant stepped across the room and picked up the phone.

"You've given us a great deal of help, Mr. Stratford. We have most of the connection from here into Canada now."

"How about back south?" Tom asked. "What'll Matt and I get when we fly into Harrisburg, a Marielito reception committee with rifles?"

"Oh, I doubt it. I'll make a call or two when the sergeant gets off the phone, but I think we've broken this pipeline." The plainsclothesman made his calls, smiling as he hung up. "We got both the Cruz brothers about an hour ago. Satterfield tells me it was quite a haul. They were directly involved with the Medellin Cartel. There won't be any bail. You're clear for Harrisburg."

"Harrisburg? I've got a shipment for Pottstown."

"It's been rerouted. The last thing we needed was your courier driving up in the middle of the action. We notified Van Ryck this afternoon, and he arranged for another pilot to pick it up."

"I'll bet he loved that!"

"He's kind of excitable, isn't he? But he cooperated. He couldn't do much else. There were a hundred kilos of cocaine in that shipment. We could have confiscated the plane, and he knew it."

"Thanks again for your help, Mr. Stratford," the plainclothesman said, shaking hands with Tom and Matt before they walked to the waiting plane.

22

Tom slid into the left-hand seat of the Cessna. Both engines caught, and the craft moved forward, trundling toward Taxiway Bravo. Matt paused on the end of the ramp while Stratford keyed the mike. "Flying Dutchman 2407, ready for taxi."

"Roger, Flying Dutchman, you're cleared for taxi." The voice paused for a moment. "Good job, guys!"

"Thanks," Tom said. They crossed the runway and turned left. Matt took his feet off the brakes, and the 310 moved forward. He turned the craft onto the runway. As he pushed the throttles forward smoothly, the plane quickly gained speed. They were airborne and turning, following tower instructions. Matt kept the nose up as they climbed steadily to their altitude. Once there, Matt trimmed the controls. When the 310 settled at 180 knots, on course for Harrisburg, Matt relaxed.

Tom spoke, "You don't need much more excitement than that to make your day!"

"I'll say!"

Tom rubbed his forehead.

"Are you all right?"

"Just another one of these headaches coming on. I'm going to have to do something about them. This has gone on long enough."

"Maybe it's all the excitement."

"Something to be said for not getting involved, I guess," Tom said.

"That's what I thought you were doing, on the way up."

"I know it. Didn't feel good to have you doubting me, but I figured it was safer for you if you didn't know what was going on."

"How long have you known, Tom?"

"You brought it up, the first shipment we hauled to Buffalo."

"Clear back then? I thought you didn't believe me."

"You made a pretty good case, but I've been working things out alone for a good many years. Gets to be second nature, I guess. But when Chico asked for my help—"

"He did?"

"Yeah, when he came to see you that day. He felt responsible for involving us, since his brothers would never have known about Flying Dutchman if he hadn't told Alfredo about your flying. I told him I'd see what I could do."

"What'll happen to Chico now?"

"I don't know, Matt. He'll have to deal with his feelings about turning in his brothers. Maybe we can help him a little, but in the end, it'll be up to him."

"I guess it always is," Matt said.

The plane flew through the heavy clouds. Matt was deep in thought when Tom spoke again, "I'm sorry, Matt."

"For what?"

"I could have gotten you killed. I should have told you what was going on. We'd have done better working together, but I've gotten used to doing things alone since LeeAnn died. I've avoided taking responsibility for other people."

Matt looked at Tom, his face serious in the dim light cast by the instrument panel. "Is that why you never got married again?"

"Sure," Tom said. "Oh, I could tell you I'd never met the right person, but it'd be an excuse. *Saturday's Warrior* to the contrary, there're any number of people you could be happily married to, if you have the important things in common."

"Do you really believe that, Tom?"

"Yep. You might be a little different person married to one person than if you'd married another, but if you're going in the same direction, eternally, and you want to share a life, you can make it work."

"What about love?"

"Are we talking about love, or desire? You can feel desire for someone you don't even like. But if you can't like someone, you can't really love them. Love is something you learn as you go along."

"What about your wife?"

"You mean, did I love her? You'd better believe it! We had a good life together, and it would have gotten better. At first, I figured life wasn't worth living without her. After a while I knew different. I could've gotten married during these past five or six years—there're lots of fine women in this church. I just didn't want to look. Now I'm glad I didn't."

Tom didn't explain. Matt looked out at the dark sky. He could see neither stars above nor lights below. They stayed on course with the VOR.

"You'd've liked LeeAnn, Matt. She's one of us."

"Us?"

"The old wild geese." Tom closed his eyes.

"You want to take a nap, Tom? Maybe that'd help."

"I think I will. I took a couple of Tylenol, but they're not doing a thing. Wake me up about fifteen minutes out of Harrisburg."

Matt flew steadily through the night. The plane droned through the thick clouds; all he had to do was maintain elevation. When he passed State College, he switched the VOR setting to Harrisburg. He checked the cockpit clock. "Tom, it's time."

Tom didn't answer. Matt reached over and shook him by

210

the shoulder. Tom stirred, struggling to come out of his heavy sleep.

"Tom, we're almost there. The cloud cover's real thick."

"Huh? Well, call for an ATIS." The pilot didn't open his eyes.

Matt keyed the mike. The ATIS report came in so poorly that Matt could hardly understand it. He tried the second radio: "Winds from the south, southwest at eighteen knots, gusting to thirty . . . Barometric pressure . . . isibility minim . . . "

"What's wrong with the radios?"

Tom struggled to sit up. "Don't know. That's how they were . . . when I had them . . . worked on . . . couple weeks ago. Haven't had . . . trouble since. Try again."

An ATIS report came over the radio, heavily interspersed with static. Matt had to listen several times to piece it together.

"Contact the tower," Tom whispered. "You'll have to . . . take . . . it in. My head . . . "

Tom slumped forward against the wheel. His weight slammed the plane into a descent. Matt jerked at his own wheel, but he couldn't pull hard enough to budge the controls. The pilot lay against the column. Matt twisted in his seat and grabbed him by the collar, put his other hand on Tom's shoulder, and yanked him back. Tom fell against the door, his head lolling against his left shoulder. He didn't move.

The plane was diving at a speed that took Matt's breath. Matt yanked the throttles back and nosed the plane up quickly. The altitude indicator, which had been unwinding like the minute hand on a broken clock, slowed. At fifteen hundred feet, it started recovering. Matt began to relax. Then the craft bucked. He'd forgotten to advance the throttles. The plane had stalled.

The bottom dropped out of Matt's stomach. His mind was totally blank. What had Tom said about stalls? He tried to remember, but nothing came. His prayer was a heartfelt plea

of pure communication, nothing but the essentials of his desperate need. His breath slowed, and his mind began to clear. He heard Tom's voice in his mind as they sat at the kitchen table.

Quickly, Matt dropped the nose and moved the throttles forward. The craft steadied and picked up speed. Cautiously, Matt resumed his climb. He knew that the mountains in the area were high enough that it was a wonder he hadn't hit one already.

He glanced at Tom. There was no change in his uncomfortable position. His eyes were closed. "Let me get him home in time," Matt pled.

He had thirty-three instruments to keep track of. He checked the vital ones on the panel in front of him. He couldn't even remember what to do about some of the others. Even at the lower altitude, the clouds were still thick. If he'd understood the ATIS, it would take an instrument landing to get him down at Harrisburg. How could he come in without the radios to guide him?

Should he try to go back? He checked the fuel gauges and understood Tom's frustration with Van Ryck. It was too far to Buffalo. There was an airport at State College, but Matt had no idea how to find it. He checked both radios. They were set on the Harrisburg frequency.

"Mayday! Mayday! Flying Dutchman 2407. Pilot incapacitated. Request permission to land."

The radio crackled, "Tower . . . IFR . . . vert . . ."

Matt keyed the mike again, working all the time to keep the craft on course, grateful for the instruments that told him whether he was upside down or rightside up. In the dense clouds, there was no other way to tell. He just had to take it on faith.

"Please repeat. Something wrong with my radios. Pilot unconscious. This is student pilot Matt Hansen, over."

"IFR condi . . . severe crosswinds . . . isibility . . . to Bal . . . "

"Repeat. Radio reception unclear. Fuel low. Pilot unconscious"—he glanced at Tom—"or dead."

What if Tom were dead? Matt couldn't bear to think about it. Tom had helped him put his feet on a very important path. If it hadn't been for Tom, he might still be shut away from people, slowly dying inside. Tom had opened his mind to life, and Matt had been able to put his own problems into perspective. I never even thanked him, he thought to himself.

Matt keyed the mike again, but no response came from the radio. Matt rechecked the frequency and tried calling on both radios. He couldn't tell whether he got through—there wasn't a crackle from either one. He had no choice but to try landing the plane alone.

His VOR worked, and thanks to Tom's persistent teaching, he could keep the 310 on course for Harrisburg. But with no help from the tower, how could he possibly descend through the heavy clouds to find the runway?

He didn't have enough training to know what to do. Matt could see the headlines. He imagined his mother at another pilot's funeral. He felt himself begin to freeze up again. His mind filled with fear. What do you do when you're too scared to do anything, Matt wondered. He knew Tom had been scared before, and surely his father must have been. "Pray," the thought came to him. "Pray."

"Father, help me get Tom out of this," Matt said as the airplane droned on through the clouds. He realized that he wasn't as frightened anymore. He felt a calm sense of confidence. He looked at Tom. The pilot still sagged against the corner of his seat, head down, arms lax in his lap. But the cold grip of fear had loosened its hold on Matt.

He checked his altimeter. It registered eight thousand feet. Matt realized that he should have begun his descent. He eased the throttles back as he pushed the column forward and dropped the nose. His speed dropped to 140 knots. The altimeter unwound steadily. Sensing that he wasn't descending rapidly enough, he dropped the nose further and pulled back on the throttles. The altimeter unwound more quickly as the plane descended through the sky.

He peered blindly through the clouds. Harrisburg was a busy airport. What if other planes were near him? What if he had come in too soon and was diving into Blue Mountain? He pulled back on the column, but the impulse to continue descending was too strong to ignore.

Reluctantly, Matt dropped the nose of the plane once more. He'd have to chance it sometime—his fuel gauges told him that. The plane descended as Matt cut his speed to 120, put on half flaps, and dropped the landing gear into place. Heavy ropes of fog nearly masked the lighted TMI cooling towers. Winds buffeted the plane as Matt flew over them. His mouth was dry; he couldn't even swallow.

Well west of the Susquehanna River, he made his final approach, hoping the tower had heard him before the radios failed.

The green-and-white beacon pierced the dark. Runway lights broke through the low clouds. Fog arose from the nearby river. It was so thick that Matt couldn't see the far end of the runway. Wind shook the plane, and fear gripped him again. His stomach twisted, and his throat closed. "Father, I can't do it," he prayed.

For just a moment, he felt a hand resting on his right hand, helping him adjust the throttles. The feeling of reassurance was so strong that Matt knew he wasn't alone. The warmth of a large hand rested on his shoulder, and other eyes than his peered through the fog.

Crosswinds rocked the 310 as their speed slowed. Matt crossed the river, rushing toward the runway. His hand turned the wheel to tilt the upwind wing. "Keep your wing down, or you'll lose it."

Matt couldn't tell whether it was Tom's voice or his father's, but the love and concern in the voice were so strong that Matt knew he wasn't bringing the plane in alone. His feet made corrections with the rudder to keep the plane's approach centered on the foggy runway. Matt remembered his landing lights. He switched them on and dropped toward the waiting runway. His lights rotated into position just as he passed over the end markers.

The right wheel touched the ground, then the left. He dropped the nose, and the forward wheel contacted the surface. He was down!

"Good job, Matt." It was Big Matt's voice. "Take care of Tom; he's one of us." The warm feeling of protection left as the 310 coasted down the runway toward the taxiway to the cargo area. Matt felt cold and drained. His hands began to shake as he tried the radios again. Nothing.

A "Follow Me" truck pulled out of the gloom, lights flashing. Matt followed it to the cargo area where an ambulance waited near the fire engines. Matt parked the plane. The ambulance sped forward, lights blinking, as Matt cut the switches. By the time his trembling hand had inserted the gustlock, someone had climbed on the wing. Matt leaned across Tom and unlocked the door.

The med-tech reached inside, felt Tom's pulse. "He's alive. Let's get him out of here. Help me with his feet."

The med-tech heaved, grunting from the strain. Matt kept Tom's feet clear of the controls. man appeared on the wing, and they pulled Tom from the plane. They laid him on a waiting stretcher and lowered it to the ground.

Matt jumped down as Tom was being lifted into the ambulance. A uniformed man waited for Matt. He led him to a car. They climbed inside as the fire engines drove away.

"Why did you come in?" the driver demanded. "The tower told you to divert to Baltimore."

"I couldn't hear the tower," Matt said. "There wasn't enough fuel to get to Baltimore anyway. I couldn't have landed there without the radios. I couldn't even get an ATIS for Baltimore."

The security stared at him, astonished. "No radios! How'd you get down in one piece?"

"I had help."

"You sure must have." He slammed the car door. "Visibility's so bad we closed the airport an hour ago!"

<h1 align="center">23</h1>

THE SECURITY OFFICER INTRODUCED HIMSELF AS CORPORAL MAXWELL. "Where can I take you?"

"Huh? Oh, the truck's over by the gate." Matt pointed. "Where'd they take Tom?"

"Harrisburg Hospital."

Matt climbed from the car. He reached into his pocket for the keys. His hand came up empty. "Oh, my gosh! Tom's got the keys."

"I'll run you over," Corporal Maxwell said. "They'll need to talk to you."

"Thanks." Matt climbed back into the car.

They moved cautiously through the wind-whipped fog up Highway 283 into Harrisburg, turned up Second Street, circled the hospital, and left the car at the curb, lights flashing. As they got out of the car, Corporal Maxwell lifted a hand against the thinning fog. "At this rate we'll be able to reopen the airport soon. It's a shame the fog didn't lift an hour ago. It would have saved you a lot of grief."

Matt smiled, thinking of the warm hand on his shoulder, the approving voice in his mind. "It would have been a whole lot easier," he agreed. But what he would have missed! "Thank you, Father," he said silently.

They stopped at the desk in the emergency room.

"I'm Matt Hansen. I'm looking for Tom Stratford."

The nurse checked a paper in front of her. "He's back in three."

217

"Can I go back? I'm his copilot."

"Were you with him when he became ill?"

"He sure was!" said Corporal Maxwell. "Eight thousand feet up."

"You'd better. The doctor will want to talk with you."

"Let us know what happens," the security officer said. "I've got to get back."

Matt walked between rows of curtained alcoves. He pushed aside the curtain to the third cubicle and ducked inside. Tom lay on a narrow bed, surrounded by people and machines. The doctor looked up.

"Who're you?" he demanded.

"Matt Hansen. I was flying with Tom. Is he going to be all right?"

"It's too early to say. Can you tell me what happened before he became unconscious?"

"We were flying out of Buffalo when he got a real bad headache. He had taken a couple of Tylenol, but they didn't work, so I told him to take a nap. He used to sleep about twenty minutes and feel rested. I thought maybe it'd help, but when I tried to wake him, I couldn't."

"How long ago was that?"

"Oh, about a quarter hour out of Harrisburg." Matt looked at the clock. "Maybe an hour ago. He sort of woke up for a minute, said something about the radios, then slumped forward. I couldn't get him to wake up at all."

"Was his speech slurred?"

"It was kind of faint, but it was clear enough."

"Did he complain of dizziness, or weakness in his arms or legs?"

"No. Just a real bad headache. He's had them lately. He said he was going to get it checked."

"He should have."

218

"He'd just had his physical two months ago. Everything was fine then."

"No history of high blood pressure?"

"Not that I know of," Matt said. "But I don't think they'd have let him fly commercially if he had had high blood pressure."

"We'll want to see that physical as soon as possible, but I don't think we have a cerebral hemorrhage. His blood pressure's normal enough now." He turned to the nurse. "I want a CAT Scan ordered."

"Can I stay with him?" Matt asked.

"Wait outside. You can go with him up to Radiology in a few minutes."

Matt stepped backward through the curtain. He slumped on a chair in the emergency waiting room and held his head in his hands. He could never remember being so tired in his life. The clock above the nurse's desk said ten to five. He'd better call his mom.

"Where's the phone?"

"Right out that door, by the elevators," the nurse replied.

The phone rang half a dozen times before Nancy picked it up.

"Mom, I'm at Harrisburg Hospital."

Her voice sharpened. "Are you all right?"

"I'm fine, Mom. It's Tom."

"What's wrong with Tom?" Anxiety brought her wide awake.

"They don't know yet. He had another one of those headaches coming into Harrisburg. He passed out, and they brought him over here in the ambulance." He'd tell her the full story after she arrived.

"I'll be right over," she said.

"Call the bishop, Mom. Tom needs a blessing."

"I will. Maybe I could drop John off there, or maybe — no, I can't take him to the hospital."

"Just call the bishop, Mom. He'll know what to do."

"Where are you now?"

"I'm at the emergency room, but they're going to take Tom upstairs to do a CAT Scan. Just ask at the desk. They'll tell you where to go." He felt a little odd telling his mother what to do.

"I'll be there as soon as I can."

Nearly thirty minutes had passed before Matt's mother walked into the waiting room. "I've never driven to Harrisburg so quickly in my life. Is the bishop here?"

"Not yet, but he had farther to come. Where's John?"

"Luckily, Mrs. Bare's kitchen light was on when I went downstairs. Her husband's shift starts at six. I called her, and she said to bring John over. He's asleep on her couch. Bless her, she's picked up a lot of pieces for me this winter. Where's Tom?"

"In there," Matt motioned.

Bishop Adams walked through the double doors, with Brother Jones at his side. "How's Tom?"

"I don't know," Matt said.

The bishop stepped over to the desk. "I'm Bishop Bruce Adams, Tom Stratford's minister. May we go back?"

"Of course."

The doctor stopped them at the entrance to the cubicle.

"I'm his bishop. May we see him?"

The doctor hesitated.

"We'd like to bless him as soon as possible," the bishop said.

"I don't think he's ready for the Last Rites," the doctor said, but he motioned the nurse out of the cubicle. "Be as quick as you can."

When the bishop and Brother Jones had finished, an orderly wheeled Tom's gurney to the elevator. Matt and his mother followed them upstairs.

For the next few days, Matt and his mother traded off. One watched John while the other stayed with Tom. He spent several days in ICU before being transferred to the neurology floor. John was thoroughly disgusted at the whole process. "Why can't I see Tom?" he asked Matt repeatedly.

"It's the rules. You have to be twelve."

"That's dumb!"

"They're afraid kids might carry germs."

"I don't have any germs. I'm never sick."

"John, if you bug me one more time, I'm going to get violent! I didn't make the rule, the hospital did. Don't gripe at me; I can't change it."

"But I want to see Tom."

They were back to square one. Matt was glad when Cindi called the Saturday after New Year's. "Why don't you let me pick John up? I'll take him to the movies and bring him home for supper. You can come get him here."

"You don't have to ask twice!"

After Cindi picked John up, Matt took Tom's pickup over to the hospital. His mother was sitting in a vinyl arm chair in the corner of the room. Tom was awake but quiet.

"What are you doing here?" she asked.

"Cindi took John to the movies, so I thought I'd come over too."

Tom smiled. "Seems kind of strange to see you both at the same time."

"How're you feeling today?"

Tom grinned. "I thought I had a headache before!"

"You know Tom," Nancy said. "He'll joke when the roof falls in."

"Nan, I've got to. Here I am flat on my back. I'm forty-six years old, and I'm out of a job again. It looks as though I'll be that way for quite a while. I've got to find something to laugh about."

221

"Well, I don't feel much like laughing," Nancy said, "but I'm grateful the tumor wasn't malignant."

"Out of a job?" Matt asked.

"I told Van Ryck to take me off the payroll. He can't afford to hold my job for me. The freight's got to move. I couldn't promise him I'd ever be able to fly again."

There was a knock on the door. Matt walked over and opened it. Dr. Samuels and Chico stood in the hall. "Come on in," Matt said.

"How are you?" Dr. Samuels asked.

Tom stuck out his hand. Dr. Samuels shook it.

"Hi, Chico," Tom said. "How you doing?"

"Very well," Chico said. "Dr. Samuels asked me to stay with him until I go to college. I help with Michael, and Dr. Samuels helps me study for my ACTs."

"That's great!" Matt said.

"I understand you had an exciting time in Buffalo," Dr. Samuels said.

"Little ruckus, not much," Tom said.

"A little ruckus, my foot!" Matt objected. "He saved my life."

"My own fault for getting you into trouble," Tom said. "I ought to have known Morrison better."

"It was my fault," Chico said. "I should have told you that my brothers were violent men."

"Since you can't agree who's to blame," Nancy said, "I'll put my two cents worth in. When someone's intent on doing something wrong, it's not other people's fault if he does it. When you make your choice, you choose your consequences. Morrison chose, and so did your brothers, Chico. You tried to do what was right, and none of this was your fault."

"I hope my mother will think so."

"She will, and so will your father," Nancy said.

"What I want to know is how you landed the plane by yourself," Dr. Samuels said, "since the radios weren't working."

"This may sound weird to you, Dr. Samuels, but I had help landing."

"I thought you were unconscious, Tom."

"Oh, I was."

Dr. Samuels looked puzzled.

"My dad was a pilot," Matt began. "He was killed test flying an F-15 when I was about eleven. I didn't want anything to do with planes after he was killed. I played football."

Matt sighed and looked down at his leg. "This last summer," he went on, "when I hurt my leg, I knew it was the end of my football career. There wasn't anything in the world I was good at but football—"

"Except mathematics," Chico interrupted.

"Well, yeah, but I wasn't thinking about that then. I was too mad. I spent all my time sitting in my room making model airplanes. Then I met Tom. He started taking me flying."

Matt grinned at Tom and tapped him on the shoulder. "It was as though my whole world opened up. That's when I met you, Chico. Remember when we got to talking about your father at lunch that day?"

"I remember," Chico said. "You told me my father cared about what I was doing. I wondered about that since my father's dead."

"Makes sense to me," Tom said. "If you believe someone lives after his death, why wouldn't he care about the people he loved when he was here?"

"An interesting metaphysical point," Dr. Samuels said. "But what does that have to do with your landing?"

Matt described the final flight, leaving out none of the details of interest to a pilot: "When Tom passed out, he fell forward against the controls and threw the plane into a steep descent. After I pulled him off, I stalled the plane trying to gain altitude. By then I was so scared I really froze up. I was afraid Tom was dead. I couldn't remember what to do. All I could do was pray."

223

Matt was silent, reliving the terror in his mind.

"What happened then?" Chico asked.

"I calmed down and began remembering what Tom had taught me. I might have done okay except for the radios. I knew I couldn't land in the fog without them, and I got scared all over again. I began praying even harder."

He paused, then looked straight at Dr. Samuels, "My father was there, helping me. I felt his hand, and I heard his voice. I know I had help landing." Matt smiled ruefully. "I sure fell apart after I was on the ground, though."

Both Chico's and Tom's eyes were bright with unshed tears. Dr. Samuels looked thoughtful. "You believe that God answered your prayers by sending your father to help you?"

Matt nodded. "I really do. I can't describe the feeling when he was there, but I sure felt it."

Dr. Samuels was silent.

After a few moments, Nancy stirred. "How's Michael, Dr. Samuels?"

"He's better. Cindi brought my wife some literature from her sister's biochemist. It's very interesting. We may be able to do more for him than we thought."

"I hope so," Nancy said.

"How long do you expect to be hospitalized, Tom?" Dr. Samuels asked.

"Couple more days. They really run you in and out."

"What are your plans?"

"Haven't decided yet. I was telling Matt, I'm out of a job again. I'll have to look around."

"You could go back to teaching." Dr. Samuels stood up. "Let me know how I can help."

"I will, Stewart. Thanks for coming."

"What *are* you going to do?" Matt asked after Chico and Dr. Samuels had left.

"It's a cinch I won't be flying five nights a week. I think I'd like running a fixed base operation. You know, fuel and flying services at a small airport. Give a few lessons to keep my license up. Maybe it's time for the FBO I was telling you about. I've been saving for a down payment for quite a while."

"Why don't you look into it?" Nancy asked.

"I have been right along. Friend of mine sent me an ad just a couple of weeks ago. I'm a bit short of what I need."

"Tom, I could put some money into it. Matt left a fair amount. I've got what's left in CDs."

Tom silent, thinking about it. "What do you think of Arizona?" he finally asked.

"Arizona? I never thought much about it. Why?"

"FBO I'm thinking about is in a little town in southeastern Arizona, Sierra Vista, down by Fort Huachucua. What would you think about that?"

"Is it a good place for an FBO?" Nancy asked.

"The FBO's doing great. The owner wants to retire."

The nurse's aide came in with Tom's dinner. She cranked up the bed and swung the table into position.

"We'll leave now," Nancy said.

Tom reached for her arm as she passed the bed. "You coming back tonight?"

"If you want me to."

"You'd better believe it!" Tom said.

Nancy nodded. She and Matt walked out of the hospital into the winter dusk.

"Let's get a pizza," Matt said. "I'll leave Tom's truck in the parking lot."

A few minutes later, they were seated inside the pizzeria. Matt sipped his root beer while they waited for their order. "So you and Tom are getting married?"

"We haven't even talked about it."

"Mom," Matt said, "I think you guys just did!"

Nancy stared at the wall. She finally gave a laugh. "I always said I didn't want candlelight dinners! How would you feel about it?"

"Oh, I think you should. Tom's one of us."

[End of Book One]